Accidental Trifecta

Masters of the Prairie Winds Club
Book Six

by Avery Gale

Copyright © October 2015 by Avery Gale
ISBN 978-1-944472-13-9
All cover art and logo © Copyright 2015 by Avery Gale
All rights reserved.

The Masters of the Prairie Winds Club® and Avery Gale®
are registered trademarks

Cover Design by Jess Buffett
Published by Avery Gale

Thank you for respecting the hard work of this author.

This is a work of fiction. Names, places, characters and incidents either are the product of the author's imagination or are used fictitiously and any resemblance to any actual persons, living or dead, organizations, events or locales are entirely coincidental.

No part of this book may be reproduced, stored in a retrieval system, or transmitted by any means without the written permission of the author and publishing company.

WARNING: The unauthorized reproduction or distribution of this copyrighted work is illegal. Criminal copyright infringement, including infringement without monetary gain, is investigated by the FBI and is punishable by up to 5 years in federal prison and a fine of $250,000.

If you find any books being sold or shared illegally, please contact the author at avery.gale@ymail.com.

Dedication

To my readers: You are the reason I enjoy writing so much. Thank you for you continued kindness and support. I appreciate each and every one of you!!!

Prologue

Twenty-five years ago...

CARL PHILLIPS SAT on the timeworn walnut bench outside the Headmaster's Office wondering how he'd managed to fall so far in such a short amount of time. Unfortunately the answer was crystal clear, no matter how hard he tried to pretend otherwise. The narrow slats of the wooden floor were cool beneath his bare feet despite the fact it was late May. The well-worn boards were polished daily, reflecting the soft lighting from the wall sconces. St. Andrew's School for Boys had a long tradition of setting the unruly teens of New England's *old money* families on the straight and narrow path to "proper behavior". The first time Carl saw *The Stepford Wives*, he'd been sure the writer must have been a St. Andrew's graduate, even though there were obvious differences, it was also a frightening accurate portrayal of what Carl saw played out all around him each and every day.

His biggest fear had always been conformity, but it had been laid out so prominently in his future, his view of everything else was overshadowed by those expectations. St. Andrew's was the answer to the age-old dilemma faced by so many in his parents' social circle that there was absolutely no way he was going to come out of this unscathed. Even if the "prick with the stick dick" as Mr.

Richards was known, let him off with a warning—which was about as likely as Carl wearing a pink tutu into the dining hall, his parents would hear about tonight's "incident" as it was being called. *Incident. Yeah, right.* In his view, incidents were isolated occurrences, and even though it hadn't happened often, tonight wasn't the first time either.

Thinking back over the past two years, Carl felt his stomach clench as the erotic images flashed through his mind. Turbulence and confusion were the only words he could find that even came close to describing the feelings and it was unfamiliar territory for his normally well-ordered mind. He prided himself on his ability to solve problems, ordinarily he could solve any puzzle put in front of him, but his conflicting feelings about this topic were far beyond his grasp. It didn't matter how many times he's tried to make sense of the conflict that had clouded his mind for the past twenty-two months—it just didn't make any sense. *Nothing about it fits anything I've ever known.* With the wooden bench beneath him, Carl shook his head sending his shaggy blond hair over his forehead to tease the tips of his sun-bleached eyelashes. He needed to stop trying to unravel the past and concentrate on how he was going to get through the next few weeks of school—unless they kicked him out, and that seemed more and more likely by the minute.

Chapter One

CARL PHILLIPS LOOKED around Kyle and Kent West's large office. Christ, the room was bigger than his last off-base apartment. Most of the team was present—seated in various spots around the room, including their single female member. But if Carl was going to place bets, he would bet Jen McCall would be darting out of the room at any moment. It was fairly obvious the stunning blonde was pregnant, but as far as he knew, she and her husbands hadn't made an official announcement yet. When she looked up and saw him looking in her direction, she made a half-assed attempt to smile, but it was as if she was afraid to move any more than necessary. He remembered hearing about Gracie McDonald's pregnancy, evidently it had been a torturous ride, and he hoped Jen's went smoother.

Most of the men lounging around the cavernous room had been in the Special Forces at the same time, and Carl had served with most of them. He considered every man in the room a friend—but that didn't mean he wasn't going to turn down this assignment if the scuttlebutt he'd been hearing was true. He didn't know Dr. Cecelia Barnes, nor did he wish her to come to harm, but the thought of being in the same room with Cameron Barnes again sent pinpricks of something to close to fear racing through him. His fear wasn't of the man himself, it was of who Carl had once been in his presence, and Carl was smart enough to avoid exposing his throat to a wolf more than once.

As he sat to the side watching everything unfold, Carl tried to sort through his feelings, but they were such a muddled mess it was difficult. He understood the excited adrenaline-fueled anxiety that accompanied particularly dicey missions, hell, he'd thrived on that high during his years as a SEAL. But this was something else entirely. This was a jolt of pure awareness, and it was far more dangerous.

Carl had spent the better part of his entire adult life trying to push Cameron Barnes from his memories...struggling to not let the man's face surface in his mind when his best friend, Peter Weston, was near. As an empath, Peter often heard or saw what was happening in the minds of those near him, particularly anyone with whom he shared a particular bond. Carl had worked hard over their years as partners to build a fortress around his memories of Cameron. But he wasn't sure how long he'd be able to maintain that mental shield if he folded under Kyle West's skillful manipulation. *God the man missed his calling. He really should have been a fucking politician.*

Kyle was presenting the case information in the straightforward, no nonsense way they were all accustomed to, but his eyes kept darting toward Carl. The pictures on the large screen to Kyle's right showed pictures of Dr. Barnes, her clinic, the home she shared with her family, her husband's ultra-exclusive sex club, and finally—Cameron Barnes. Just looking at the man's photograph sent a white-hot surge of electricity up and back down his spine. The heat had literally traveled at the speed of light until settling squarely in his cock. *Just fucking perfect, sitting here thinking about working with one of my team leaders' buddies and I sprout a major woody...just brilliant, Phillips.*

The final picture was of the Barnes' sleeping daughter, Chloe. Even though Carl knew his new boss had left the sleeping infant's picture on the screen deliberately, it didn't lessen its impact. Cameron Barnes had a dark past...a very dark past tainted by his exposure to the world on a level most people only see in the movies or on the evening news. Cameron had, at one time or another, worked for almost every alphabet agency the United States had ever managed to dream up, not to mention those of more governments than the average American could name. He'd been the "go to guy" for missions requiring such a variety of skills, Cam was often referred to as the MacGyver of the spy world. He was fearless, brilliant, and deadly.

Looking up, Carl met Peter's gaze and knew in that instant he'd let his guard down for the microsecond his friend had needed. Peter raised a brow in question but didn't voice the inquiry—he didn't have to. The intense look on Peter's face told Carl they would be having the conversation he'd always dreaded—and that it would likely occur sooner rather than later. Peter Weston was one of the least judgmental men Carl had ever known. He'd always wondered if Peter was open-minded because of the overload of information he received every day or because the man's gift of insight into the hearts and minds of others kept him from judging people harshly until they crossed some "impossible to define" boundary of personal and ethical behavior. Peter Weston's hypersensitivity to extreme violence kept him out of combat situations most of the time, but his contributions to the intelligence gathering the teams depended on had been immeasurable.

Just as Kyle turned his gaze toward Carl, a quick movement to his left caught everyone's attention. Jen

McCall was standing unsteadily on her feet, her eyes darting around the room as if assessing the most expedient route of escape. Her pretty face had gone a pasty shade of green that made Carl think of the rundown medical facilities of the Middle East. Her hand was pressed firmly against her mouth and beads of sweat popped out over her face and arms right in front of his eyes. *She's never going to get out of here in time without help.* The thought had no sooner moved through his mind than Sam McCall scooped his petite wife into his arms and made his way quickly out of the office.

His brother stood and flashed everyone a guilty grin. Sage was younger and less intense, and his boyish demeanor often fooled targets into underestimating him, but the man was every bit as deadly in a fight as any operative Carl had ever met. "Guess this confirms the rumors that have been circulating around the club. We'd planned to explain at the end of this meeting why we are pulling out of the assignment, but I think things speak for themselves." When Sage's gaze met his, Carl knew he was fucked seven ways to Sunday, "We appreciate the fact we're a part of a team that is more family-oriented than most. Thanks for stepping up even when I sense for some reason it isn't going to be easy for you."

Yeah, you could fucking say that again. Craptastic.

Sage stepped through the doorway, but stuck his head back in and smiled ruefully, "We'll give your housekeeper a heads up, and ummm...pay for the rug." Carl had to hold back his laugh because the man had turned a nice shade of green himself. "Oh, and tell your women she's seven weeks along—I know they'll ask and I don't want twenty text messages." As soon as the door closed, the room erupted into laughter and the occasional gagging noise. It was good to know their frat mentality was never far below the surface.

CAMERON BARNES STARED down at the letter laying in the center of his desk, but he wasn't really seeing it. It didn't matter, he'd read it so many times he knew each word by heart. He'd known better than to tempt fate by feeling safe. The life he'd led, the enemies he'd made, the demons he'd befriended, wouldn't be so easily cast aside, and he'd been foolish to think he'd come through it all unscathed. But having it so clearly pointed out had shaken him to his core. Cam had completed missions no other operative would even consider without even hesitating, but his hands had shaken so badly when he'd first opened the messenger's envelope he'd been forced to place the letter on his desk just to read it.

After alerting his staff and sending additional security to Cecelia's clinic, Cam had called the only men he trusted with the lives of his wife and child. Their first conversation had been short, as he'd known it would be. Kent and Kyle West had promised to give their team a quick sit-rep and have them on their way within the hour. They hadn't been sure which two-man team would be coming, and Cam hadn't thought to ask why until Kyle had called back to let him know help was on the way.

"I'd recommend assigning one man to CeCe and the other to the club. Since there weren't any direct threats to Chloe, I really believe Adam and Camille can easily protect her, and their vested interest only strengthens their conviction to keep her safe. Let Fischer know we're sending his brother for a visit. He'll be able to use their sibling connection as a cover for visiting the club. Peter's gifts aren't as strong as Fischer's, but he is a people magnet and hides his gifts better than his siblings." Cam agreed. He'd met all three Weston brothers and understood exactly what Kyle was talking about. Peter was far more discreet than either his older or his younger brother, and most people who met him had no idea how much he learned about them from a simple handshake.

Cam knew only a handful of Peter's commanding officers had known about his abilities, and they'd worked hard to utilize his gifts without compromising his safety. Hell, if *the company* had ever gotten wind of what Peter and his brothers could do, there'd be no end to their recruiting efforts. The only other man who'd been more valuable behind the scenes was Micah Drake. Micah was usually referred to as the computer guru or hacker to the gods—depending on your prospective. Smiling for the first time in hours, Cam couldn't help but wonder how the Wests had managed to lure so many of the SEAL teams' best and brightest right out from under the noses of the brass. Cam had offered the Wests his advice on several different *missions* they'd taken since they'd begun contract work. He'd advised them to walk away from a few also. *Too bad you didn't listen when you were told the same thing.* Perhaps he wouldn't have brought the dregs of the world to his front door if he'd been thinking about his future instead of continually running from the past.

Now, after all those years spent convincing himself he'd made the right decision by walking away from the man he hadn't seen since that night twenty-five years ago, they were going to be face to face in a matter of minutes. Cam had known the minute Kyle had said Peter was on his way who the second man was. Peter Weston and Carl

Phillips had been partners since BUDs and they'd joined the Wests' team at the same time, so it was a no-brainer.

Cameron shook his head as he remembered how he'd spent hours convincing the Headmaster that he alone, was responsible for the "isolated incident" and then walked right past his friend without uttering a word. Cam had made certain that by the time Carl returned to their room, he'd be gone. He'd lived off-campus for the last few weeks of school, enlisted in the military, and skipped the graduation ceremony. His family had ignored him for years, and Cam was convinced they'd only "offered" to put aside their differences because of Cecelia. Clearly having a renowned pediatric surgeon in the family had gone miles farther than a mercenary who'd traveled the world, pledging his loyalty to whoever offered him the most lucrative deal. Their offer had been too little and far too late, he hadn't even returned their call.

Cameron tried very hard to always be honest in his business dealings and even more so in his self-appraisal. He'd done so many things he was proud of, but he'd also done too many that he wished he could forget. One of his biggest regrets had always been not talking to Carl Phillips before leaving St. Andrew's, he'd owed his friend that much. When he'd learned Carl had refused to let Cam take the blame alone and had been expelled, he'd been angry, but impressed with the young man's integrity. Carl's dad had eventually secured his diploma, but the damage to their relationship had been permanent according to mutual friends.

Taking a deep breath, Cameron turned toward the large black steel framed mirror to his side. He'd built a small private sitting room that was only accessible through the hidden door along the side of the enormous piece of glass. Standing on the other side offered a crystal clear view into the office, and he'd used it more times than he could count for various reasons. He planned to use it again when he interviewed nanny candidates, but he'd only needed to schedule one. He'd arranged their meeting for the next day, but that plan appeared to be on hold for now. Damn his timing, he'd been waiting months to find a submissive that would be a good candidate for the position—he hated having a woman in his home that didn't understand his and Cecelia's lifestyle. *Hell, I'd do the interview tonight if she happens to show up at the club and is willing.* Above everything else, he hated the fact his sweet slave was becoming all too accustomed to wearing clothing in their home. He'd always insisted she remain naked unless he gave her very specific permission to cover herself. And since most of their friends were also club members, the occasions where he'd let her dress were few and far between.

But today the mirror only had one purpose, reflecting the image of a man Cam barely recognized. The one staring back at him looked exhausted and far older than the one he'd seen there yesterday. *Yeah, seeing pictures of the two women who are your heart and soul printed beneath the words recounting your career tends to age people...quickly.*

Turning back to his desk, he leaned back and waited. The irony of his current situation wasn't lost on him. He sat waiting for the man he'd considered his very best friend...the one he'd walked away from...the one he'd never even looked at as he stalked from Mr. Prick-with-a-Stick-Dick's office...the man whose friendship had challenged everything Cameron had thought he believed in. He stared across the room with unseeing eyes. The one man he'd let down more than any other, was the same man he was about to entrust with his most sacred possessions. Karma really could be a cruel bitch.

Chapter Two

CARL STOOD OUTSIDE the door to Cameron Barnes' office and wondered once again how he'd managed to get himself in such a predicament. Thinking back over the past few hours it was clear he'd been steamrolled by fate once again. He understood why Sam and Sage had pulled out of the op, he would do the same thing if he ever managed to get his life together enough to find a woman willing to put up with his moody self. But understanding the reasons and being happy about it were far different.

The trip to Houston had been relatively quiet. Peter had obviously sensed Carl wasn't yet ready to talk about the reason he hadn't wanted to take this assignment, but Carl knew his reprieve would be short-lived. Fischer Weston was an even stronger empath than his older brothers, and his questioning look when they'd shaken hands was all it had taken to remind Carl that shielding wasn't easy with Fischer. The brothers had taken off for the club's main room to talk since they would be working together at Dark Desires and Carl had been directed to "Master C's" office. He'd found the ornate door easily enough—but finding it and being ready to confront the man whose face still haunted him were two entirely different things.

CAM MIGHT HAVE *thought* he was ready to see the best friend he'd ever had walk through the door, but his confidence had far outweighed reality. Carl Phillips had been devastatingly handsome at seventeen, but hell, he probably stopped traffic now. He was taller than Cam remembered and his blond hair was slightly darker than it had been twenty-five years ago, but Carl's eyes were still the same remarkable shade of blue that reminded him of the sparkling waters of the Caribbean Sea. Their greeting was polite but awkward, and the few seconds of silence that followed made Cam appreciate the thousands of times he'd used silence to make subs squirm in their seats. *Yeah, a little taste of my own medicine and it's damned humbling.*

It felt as if the air had been sucked from the room, and a pin dropping to the floor would have easily been heard in the vacuum. Cam's mind flashed back to their encounters before that fateful night and felt himself freefall into the sensory memory of Carl Phillips. The way his skin felt beneath Cam's fingertips, the scent of his soap, the way gooseflesh raced over the tan skin covering his back when Cam gripped his narrow waist. Taking a deep breath in an effort to refocus his attention on the present, Cam was relieved to see the man standing in front of him appeared to be as affected by their reunion as he was.

Why had he run? Why hadn't he stayed and fought for what they'd had? He'd abandoned a young man that had been far more innocent than Cam had been—hell, he'd essentially thrown his friend to the wolves and never looked back. Once again, shame washed over him in a hot wave but he pushed it back because going there wasn't going to protect Cecelia or Chloe. Standing up, he walked around his desk and shook Carl's hand. "Thanks for coming. It's good to see you again." He gestured to the chair in front of his desk, "Have a seat, can I get you anything to drink?"

Carl shook his head, "No thanks, I'm good. I was happy to help Sam and Sage out, they need to stay with Jen until she's feeling better." Cam didn't miss the less than subtle message that he was here because of his teammates, not to help Cam. Returning to his seat, Cam simply turned the letter he'd been studying all day around and pushed it forward. Carl leaned forward and asked, "Is this a copy or the original? Did you already check it for prints?"

"It's the original and no I won't involve the police until I have to." He gave Carl an assessing look, but the man's mask of indifference remained solidly in place. The flair of emotion he'd seen in his blue eyes when Carl first stepped through the door had since been shuttered behind the face of a seasoned military operative. Cam suspected the look was also of a former friend who wasn't going to forgive and forget easily.

"Care to explain why you didn't at least notify the local authorities? You may regret not laying that groundwork later."

"Well, I didn't say they hadn't been notified, I just don't want them involved until I don't have any other options. You and I both know they operate under far more restrictions than we do." And wasn't that the understatement of the fucking year. He'd rarely worked inside the U.S. because the red tape involved was staggering, but he had done enough to feel sorry for the men and women who put their lives on the line each and every day despite the quagmire of bureaucratic bullshit they had to work in.

Wearing a badge in the United States wasn't an easy path to follow, despite what most people believed.

There were, in fact, several members of various law enforcement agencies on Dark Desires' membership roll, and Cam had contacted at least one from each agency after calling Kyle West. The bond between Dominants was strong, Cam knew the men wouldn't share the information until the time was right, but giving them a heads up would certainly have its advantages. Whoever sent the letter and pictures was likely still nearby, so having more people watching and listening could only help.

Cam wasn't surprised by Carl's intensity and focus, but he was surprised by the man's patience. His friend had obviously learned a lot in the years since they'd been close because he'd been much more spontaneous back then. Cam knew the man's IQ was well within the range to qualify as a Mensa, but he also knew Carl had never been particularly impressed with that piece of information. The Wests assured Cam that Carl was still one of the best strategists they'd ever met and his ability to solve puzzles was the stuff of military legend. But as a much younger man he'd been plagued by his inability to stay still—watching him now, it was difficult to believe he was the same man.

Cam had scanned the file Jax had forwarded to him containing the profiles of the operatives they had recruited. The Prairie Winds team was the cream of the crop, but it didn't seem that even the long reach of their connections had uncovered the fact he and Carl weren't strangers. Kyle and Kent had authorized the release of a file summary so Cam and CeCe would feel secure having him staying in their home—a fact he'd found amusing. It had been nice to read the bios of the other team members they'd be taking along, but it really hadn't been necessary, he trusted Jax, Micah, and the Wests implicitly. Cam had been reluctant about Carl's involvement, that was a given, but not for any of the reasons they would have assumed. At one time they'd been so close they had been able to finish one another's sentences, now he sat across from a virtual stranger who merely looked a lot like someone he'd once known.

"I assume from that answer you've contacted club members in various agencies so they'll keep their ears to the ground?" It might have sounded like a question, but Cam knew better, and when he merely nodded, Carl took a deep breath before leaning forward. "Listen, I'm here to do a job, I haven't met Cecelia yet, but she deserves my best effort. She and your daughter are innocents, this isn't their fight, and we both know it. She is also a friend to several people who are very important to me, so I want to keep her as safe as possible because being on Tobi, Gracie, and Meri's shit list doesn't appeal to me—not at all." And there it was, the first hint of humor indicating the Carl Phillips he'd once known was still inside the stoic man seated across from him.

Cam couldn't hold back his smile, "Well, for what it's worth, I think staying off Tobi's and Gracie's radars is wise, but I'm not convinced they've had enough time to corrupt Merilee just yet." He paused and then leaned forward, "Cecelia will be here momentarily. She has been my full-time slave outside of her career for several years. We've had to make some adjustments to our lifestyle since Chloe's birth that neither of us are particularly content with because we have had a live-in nanny who isn't in the lifestyle. I was supposed to interview one tomorrow before the club opened. I am hopeful that it works out, well, I'd like you to observe the interview along with Cecelia."

"I assume you are talking about watching from the room behind that mirror."

Cam didn't even try to hold back his grin, he wasn't at all surprised Carl had spotted the two-way mirror, it wasn't difficult if one knew what to look for. "Correct. I'll want your impressions about both women's reactions." He waited for a moment for recognition to hit his friend's eyes before continuing, "The young woman I'm interviewing is a trained submissive, she has the credentials to care for Chloe, and I think she'll fit in well. My only hope is we'll be able to keep her because she also appears to have caught Fischer's eye." Cam knew Peter and Carl had shared women for some time, it was a part of the dossier he'd gotten from Kent and Kyle. What he didn't know was how Carl would feel about Fischer and Peter sharing together without him, and that was exactly what he suspected would happen with Lara.

During dinner one evening, Fischer had confided that he knew there would be a woman who would bring him and his brother back together. Cam had always believed Peter had found a woman he'd thought was right, but Fischer had rejected her. His club manager hadn't shared all of the details of their differences, but Cam knew Fischer believed there would be one woman that both one of them could "read," and she'd be *the one*. Fischer had been fascinated with Lara—from the first moment he realized her thoughts weren't completely open to him. Now Cam could only hope his friend could hold off his "happily ever after" long enough for him to ensure the safety of his wife and child. *You know full well that fate is a fickle friend and you have a lot of negative slash marks on the wrong side of your tally board.*

Cam had no intention of laying all his cards on the table just yet, after all, focusing on anything other than keeping Cecelia and Chloe safe wasn't an option. Refocusing his attention, he continued, "Cecelia is well-trained, but I'm concerned this situation may well throw her into a tailspin. She has never asked for any details about what I did before we met—personally, I think she was too worried to ask."

"And you didn't make her confront that fear?" The disbelief in Carl's voice was easy to hear and Cam wouldn't have expected anything less from a trained Dom, particularly one who had at one time known him well—very well. He'd been selfish and a coward, but that wasn't something he was interested in admitting out loud, at least not to the only other person in this world he'd let down.

"She had already scheduled the next few days off, we'd planned to go out of town and Chloe is already at her aunt and uncle's. Adam Weston is married to Cecelia's older sister, Camille. Their home is very secure and Adam has taken some additional precautions. The trip we'd planned would have made protecting Cecelia very difficult without some security upgrades. I already have a team working on those but it will take them a couple of days to complete the installation of an enhanced motion detection system. In the meantime, we'll be taking a private jet to New York tonight. I've arranged for a place where the security is as top-notch as it gets. We'll spend a few days there while security upgrades are done in St. Maarten. Cecelia is probably going to be off work longer than a week, her clinic manager is working on that end of things." For the first time in his life, Cameron Barnes was essentially flying by the seat of his pants. During his career, relegating tasks to others had always been far too dangerous, and delegating had been one of the most difficult skills for him to master after becoming a civilian business owner.

He hadn't had time to fully consider all the angles, but on a soul deep level he trusted Carl Phillips. All he could do at this point was send up an impassioned plea to the Universe because even though he and Carl had both earned more than their share of negative karma, Cecelia had not. A small kernel of hope had sprouted in his heart when he'd heard Carl was coming to Dark Desires. *Is it possible he'll be as captivated by her as I am?* They'd always liked the same people when they were younger, so maybe… Just as Cam started to explain what he was planning in St. Maarten, a soft knock sounded at the door. *Well, there's no time like the present to find out if my suspicions are right.*

Chapter Three

STANDING IN THE shadows watching the activity of the club, he could almost feel the energy shift. *Yes, the package had stirred things up for sure. Maybe now Master C will start to see the truth. He should have never married that woman. He isn't being true to himself. Women are the root of everything evil.* All the teachers at school had said so and he'd listened. Craig had always listened to his teachers because their words were the only ones that could chase away the demons that wanted to fill his mind. Even now he knew he had to keep listening to the Father at church or the demons would start talking to him again, and he hated what they asked him to do. Too messy. The coopery smell of blood always made him ill. The circles of stone, the candles, the damned chanting. It was all so messy. He hated messy. No, everything needed to stay clean.

Shaking his head to throw off his straying thoughts, Craig Allen refocused on what was happening around him. He had waited years for this chance, and now that he'd finally taken it, he felt almost giddy with anticipation. He'd worked at the club for three years—three long years of waiting for the owner to recognize him. Master C still didn't realize they'd known each other years ago. Craig didn't know how long he might have waited if he hadn't been standing outside Master C's office one afternoon and overheard him discussing the possible sale of the club.

Once again, Craig was grateful he'd taken a job on the custodial staff even though he certainly didn't need the money. But agreeing to the menial position had been a stroke of genius because he'd quickly discovered service personnel were virtually invisible. And that invisibility allowed him access to each and every one of Dark Desires' inner sanctums. Being five foot seven and slender, meant he wasn't imposing enough for anyone to notice. He kept his brown hair covered with a cap most of the time, adding another layer of invisibility.

Craig watched as a man entered Master C's office, he looked familiar but he didn't know why. A short time later, Craig watched as Dr. Barnes entered the club, she looked pale and worried. *Good, perhaps she will prove to be as brilliant as everyone claims and leave while she can.*

CARL HAD BEEN trying to fit together all the pieces he was gathering but he hadn't been able to unravel the puzzling interplay between him and Cam. Riddles, codes, logic puzzles, anagrams—hell, they'd all been child's play for him as long as he could remember, but Cameron Barnes had always been the one person whose actions he'd never fully understood. Most people were boringly predictable once you'd gathered enough information, but Cam had always operated so far outside the norm there wasn't a pattern to base any prediction on. The man was holding something back—probably a lot actually, but Carl was so knocked off base and disconcerted by their meeting, he really wasn't able to sort through all the thoughts and emotions moving at the speed of light through his head.

There had been brief moments during the time since

he'd stepped into Cam's office when he'd felt a distinct connection with his former friend. But more often Carl had been simply struggling to find a lifeline in the conversation, because the man in front of him bore only the faintest whisper of resemblance to the passionate young man he'd once known. The Cameron Barnes he'd known was determined to change the world—he'd been convinced he could right all the wrongs if he just removed enough of the threats. *God, didn't we all think that when we first signed up for the Special Forces?* But Carl knew Cameron had gone considerably further in his pursuits. The man had become something of a legend in the field—he was a ghost who moved undetected in and out of countries with ease. He'd never missed a target and his abilities to steal information out from under the noses of those around him almost exceeded his reputation as an assassin. Where Carl excelled at long-range sniper shots, Cam's specialty was those kills that were up-close and personal.

The soft knock at Cam's office door brought Carl back to the moment and the brief flash of pure heat in his eyes had Carl sitting up straight in his seat. "Come." The man's one word command was all it took to bring the most exotically beautiful woman Carl had ever seen into the room. The fact she was naked sent a jolt of heat straight through his chest and even he heard his sharp intake of breath. She had her eyes cast toward the floor, but he'd still been able to catch the barest hint of an upward tilt at their corners telling him she had some Asian background, probably a generation or two back. Carl could almost feel her questions as she moved across the expanse of floor between them, but her training prevented even the smallest glance in his direction.

Carl had seen her picture during the sit-rep at Prairie

Winds, but they had failed miserably to capture the exquisite beauty of the woman kneeling at her Master's feet on the other side of the desk separating them. Carl was suddenly very grateful for the thick piece of glass that made up Cameron's desktop because he had a front row seat enabling him to study her more carefully. The long dark hair he'd originally thought was simply a dark brunette now showed a variety of dark highlights that seemed to shift like the sands of the nighttime Sahara in strong winds. He'd been enthralled the first time he'd watched the desert move beneath his feet, changing under the night sky. Finding out all the ways Mother Nature could alter the appearance of something in the dark had been mesmerizing as well as humbling.

Watching her gracefully descend into a perfect pose stole his breath. Cam hadn't been kidding when he'd referred to her as well trained, everything about her screamed perfection. The woman was a visual feast for any man and probably most women as well. Her lightly tanned skin glowed with health and something too close to fatigue for his comfort. Even from his position several feet away, Carl could see the flush of arousal begin to move over her skin leaving a rosy blush in its wake. Her spread legs gave him a breath-stealing view of her sex and the lips of her labia looked like rose petals unfurling under the sun's warmth, their color was becoming deeper and when the scent of her honey hit him, Carl felt his nostrils flare in their attempt to take in as much of the honeyed smell as possible.

By the time Carl realized how long he'd been staring—completely captivated by the vision in front of him—it was far too late to deny the effect Dr. Barnes' entrance had on him. Meeting Cam's gaze, he was relieved to see the man wasn't offended—in fact, he appeared pleased even though he was trying to bank his emotions. When Carl quirked a brow at him in question, a ghost of a smile caused the corners of Cam's lips to twitch so slightly Carl wasn't sure it had actually happened. "She's beautiful, isn't she?"

"She is gorgeous. You are a very fortunate man." Carl could hear the raspy sound of his own arousal surfacing despite his best efforts to tamp it down.

"I am, indeed." Cameron's voice was full of pride, but Carl heard the roughened tone of barely leashed dominance that most people would have missed. Then turning to his slave, Cam's voice became softer, a tone Carl doubted was the norm during their time inside Dark Desires. "Look at me, pet." When she looked up into her Master's eyes, Carl couldn't tell if hers were really that dark or if they were just fully dilated, but it didn't really matter because that look was a siren's call to a Dom. "As you know we have a problem. Someone has made the incredibly poor decision to threaten what is mine." Carl watched her eyes go glassy with unshed tears that he could only assume were a mixture of fear and uncertainty, but once again she didn't voice her worry. Since her Master hadn't asked her a question, she just blinked as if signally him that she'd heard his words. "The man sitting across from me is an old friend, he is also a member of the Prairie Winds' team. He will be staying with us at least until this is resolved." *At least? What the fuck?*

CECE HAD BEEN struggling to keep her emotions in check since she'd taken Cameron's call earlier in the day. Thank God she hadn't planned to see patients today because she wasn't sure she'd have been able to give them the attention they deserved. She had planned to finish up charting and make notes for the physicians filling in for her while she was on vacation, and even that task had proven difficult. Cam had planned the entire trip, including asking her sister and brother-in-law to care for Chloe. She'd been looking forward to the coming week for months, it was the anniversary of her collaring and spending time at their beach house in St. Maarten was always one of her favorite ways to unwind. Her surgical clinic had grown exponentially in the past two years and she often found herself so buried in work she forgot to eat. It was only a matter of time before her weight loss became an issue with her Master, he wasn't the type to miss even the most insignificant change in her body, and he was even less apt to let it go unchallenged.

The small home's wide wrap around porch with its comfortable furniture and spectacular views of the rolling waves of the Caribbean Sea was the perfect place to relax and play. The kitchen would be fully stocked by the time they arrived by the housekeeper who they'd hired several years ago to keep the place ready for visitors. But her favorite feature of the getaway was the small, but fully equipped dungeon on the lower level. The room faced the beach and when the large panel windows were opened, the entire space felt as if it joined the outdoors. The concrete floor had been stained the exact color of the beach and its rough texture only added to the illusion. Instead of the dark colors that were usually used in kink clubs, the beach playroom was a soulful blend of blues and greens with accents of all things nautical. Her Master had laughed when she'd told him how perfectly he'd met her "damsel kidnapped by a pirate" fantasy.

Cameron's ability to disguise equipment designed to torture willing submissives so it appeared to fit in any room's décor had always amazed her. She'd always considered herself a science nerd with the decorating style of a lab rat. When she'd first met Cameron Barnes he'd been on a mission in Italy while she'd been on vacation in Rome. She'd simply thought he was a rich playboy with the ability to set her entire body on fire, but his past was evidently far more complicated than the former Special Forces operative had originally copped to. CeCe had never been able to wrap her mind around the fact the man who so painstakingly surrounded her with beauty and could bring her so much pleasure with the simplest of touches had been involved in anything sinister.

The artistic side of the man always seemed incongruent with the Dom she knew so well and the former operative she'd heard whispered about during social gatherings. The only thing she knew for sure at this point was that she really didn't know anything at all about her Master's past. Mentally shaking her head at the Socrates reference, CeCe could only hope that she didn't end up drinking hemlock in the end.

CAM WATCHED THE play of emotions on his sweet slave's face and cursed the fact he was going to have to deny her beach escape for a bit. It didn't matter it would only be a short delay, he still hated breaking a promise, but in the end his pledge to protect her would *always* take precedence. He hadn't seen her this distracted in so long he'd almost forgotten what it was like to look into her obsidian eyes and see anything but passion. He knew she considered herself a scientist above all else, hell, she'd even questioned her ability to be a good mother. But Cam knew the loving, generous, and passionate woman that was really the core of her soul. Both she and her sister, Camille, had been raised in an environment that valued knowledge above all else, so it was little wonder she'd been shocked when he'd peeled back those layers to reveal the sexual woman beneath.

Skimming his fingers down the side of her face as he watched her, Cam was amazed by the fact she'd barely registered his touch. Clearly his call earlier in the day had unsettled her far more than he had anticipated. It was time to refocus her attention, and demanding she see to his pleasure certainly wasn't the most unpleasant idea he'd had today. Cecelia's submission was deeply buried beneath layer upon layer of academic and professional polish, but it was an elemental part of her soul. He'd learned over the years the smarter the submissive, the more difficult it was to get them out of their own heads, and it looked like Cecelia was going to be a challenge tonight.

Shifting his attention from Cecelia to Carl, Cam slid the only other sheet of paper on his desk over to his former friend. He watched the former SEAL's eyes widen in obvious surprise and then the burst of heat that followed a Dom's understanding of the unspoken message. Cam had never shown his love's limit list to any other Dominant, but then he'd never dreamt he'd be given the opportunity to share her with Carl Phillips either. Serendipity and fate never ceased to amaze him in spite of the fact his career had jaded him to the point things rarely surprised him.

Cam watched Carl's eyes skim the list before he leaned back in his chair. The almost imperceptible nod of his head told Cam that he'd read and understood the limits, but his quirked brow let him know the other Dom wasn't exactly sure what he was supposed to do with the information. *He'll see soon enough.* Pushing his chair back enough Cecelia would feel the loss of heat, Cam leaned back and watched her closely. Her nipples were barely peaked, she didn't appear to be wet, and her pulse was barely noticeable at the base of her slender neck—all clear indicators that her head wasn't in the right place. Letting her feel his gaze had always stirred her arousal, when none of those telltale signs appeared, Cam realized how much he missed the flushing of her skin and the small sighs she made as her mind and body sought his mastery.

Moving back so he was close once again, he cradled her chin in his palm, Cam lifted her face so he could look directly into her eyes. Once her attention was fully focused on him, he spoke softly, "Pet, I'm going to help you with the anxiety I see you struggling with, but first I want you to know how sorry I am this has happened." The tears that filled her soulful eyes made his chest tighten, straining under the guilt he'd already been feeling. Leaning forward he pressed his lips against her forehead, "I'd like nothing more than to be able to go back and change my past so I could promise you this would never happen again—but we both know that isn't possible."

"Master?" She'd spoken so softly Cam might not have even heard her if he hadn't been looking right into her sweet face. His quick nod let her know she could continue, "I wouldn't want you to change your past, because that would change who you are now. And *this* is the man I have given my life, my devotion, and my love to, so I won't ever wish for you to be someone else." Her heartfelt words slammed into Cam's chest with the force of a freight train, he didn't have any idea what he'd done to warrant her unconditional love, but he wasn't about to question the gift. Their relationship might be admired by others as an example of how rewarding a power exchange could be, but Cam was wise enough to recognize the truth. Dr. Cecelia Barnes owned his heart—she had from the moment he'd laid eyes on her. His only hope now was that he wasn't going to taint what they had with a truth he had never been brave enough to share with her.

Chapter Four

CARL WATCHED THE interplay between Master and slave, and wondered if the woman had any idea how much power she had in their relationship. He'd read her bio, knew she was incredibly intelligent, so it was likely she knew and simply didn't care. She was exactly the opposite of what he'd always considered his "type" yet everything about the woman flipped his switches.

Dr. Cecelia Barnes' dark hair and eyes made her look mysterious and her softly rounded figure made him think of cuddling beside a crackling fire. He'd make sure the room was warm enough that her bare skin wouldn't feel any chill while he memorized every square inch of her. Oddly enough her file had included a notation that she loved Richart chocolate, so he'd made a point to pick up a large box before he and Peter made their way to Dark Desires. He'd thought it odd that a dossier had contained such a trivial detail, but after seeing her, it was easy to understand. CeCe was the type of woman men wanted to care for, nurture, and spoil with anything her heart desired. There was an Old World flair to her beauty, her high cheekbones and the slight angle of her eyes pulled him in like a moth to a flame.

Cam had never spoken much about the future during the time they'd been friends. Carl had always gotten the impression his friend hadn't expected to live that long, and considering his reputation after joining the Navy, that had probably been an accurate assessment. Everything the man had done after joining the SEALs was classified and his time after leaving the teams was so buried most of the brass at the Pentagon probably weren't even aware Cameron Barnes was still alive. Carl had been hearing rumors about Cam for years, but had no way to separate the stories that were based on facts from those that had simply become tales of hero worship perpetuated by admirers.

CECE ENTERED CAM'S office and quickly moved into her usual position at her Master's side. Cam always made sure his office was the perfect temperature for her even though she was sure it was far too warm for his comfort. Looking up surreptitiously, she noted the light glistening of the tanned skin on the back of his hands and knew she'd been right. She kept her head down to maintain her posture while kneeling, but the sight of his strong fingers overlapping where his hands were clasped together pulled her attention and held her enthralled as her mind worked over all the plans they'd made for their vacation. Knowing the pleasure and pain those fingers could bring her, sent a slick flood of moisture to her pussy. Her Master never missed any sign from her body so it was only a matter of time before he smelled her arousal. But as he continued talking to the man sitting across from him, she found herself turning her thoughts inward and soon she was lost in her worries and lost track of their conversation entirely.

She wasn't unnerved by the other man in the room, and even though her Master had spoken of him, he was sitting within her peripheral vision but she kept her eyes downcast so she didn't know if she'd seen him before or not. What puzzled her was the tension she'd detected in his voice when he'd spoken, and what on earth did he mean "at least until this is resolved"? They'd never discussed adding a third to their relationship, she wasn't particularly opposed to the idea, but she'd never been one of those people who adjusted to change easily either. Reminding herself it wasn't hers to worry over, she evened out her breathing and let her mind drift. Handing over the worries of her life, outside her professional life, was one of the best parts of her submission.

CeCe wasn't naïve enough to ignore the power she had in their relationship, she knew Cameron Barnes loved her every bit or more than she loved him. He'd told her one night early in their relationship that he depended upon her "goodness" to even out his bad karma. When she'd laughed, he'd shaken his head, "I've never been more serious, pet. Your soul is free of the burdens of my past and that innocence will be safe with me forever if I can arrange it." They'd been drinking wine and she'd attributed his admission to the alcohol's effect, but the next night he'd collared her and proposed. She'd barely managed to hold him off until her sister could help her plan the small ceremony, and through it all she'd gotten the sense he worried she would change her mind.

Most people saw their union as peculiar, but it worked for them…or at least she'd thought it was working. Now that she considered his words, she wondered if there had been more to them. He'd referred to the man as an old friend, but the only friend she'd ever heard Cam mention was Jax McDonald. When she felt her Master's breath brush against her ear she realized he'd leaned close while she'd been lost in thought. "I know you have been looking forward to our trip to the beach, but in order for us to keep you safe I'm having the security system upgraded and it won't be ready for a couple of days."

Oh fuck me. Don't cry...don't cry...don't cry. She hadn't even considered the fact the security problem Cam had mentioned on the phone might disrupt their plans. Blinking furiously she managed to hold back the tears, but just barely and there wasn't a chance in hell her ultra-attentive—often to the point she wanted to pull her hair out—Master wouldn't notice. He held her chin between his fingers and looked down into her eyes and when she dropped her gaze, he tightened his hold in warning. "Don't hide your pain from me, pet. I own it as much as I own your pleasure. It's all mine, do you understand?"

"Yes, Sir." CeCe knew her voice shook, but his reminder that he wanted all of her, even the pieces she didn't believe were as attractive, kept her from caring.

"Good. Now, I am going to break our usual way of doing things and give you a brief rundown of what I have planned for this evening. We're going to play a bit now because I need to feel your hot mouth wrapped around my cock. You're going to show our friend just how much you love pleasing your Master. During that time, he's going to have the opportunity to pleasure you, but you will not come until one of us gives you permission to do so. You will obey him as you would me, is that clear?"

"Yes, Sir." There was more strength in her response this time and she wasn't sure if it was because Cam had given her time to settle, or if it was Tobi's and Gracie's voices replaying in her head as they expounded on the mind shattering orgasms they achieved at the hands of their two Masters. Her two friends had bragged and boasted about how fantastic the sex was with two men until CeCe had wanted to throttle them both. She wasn't jealous by nature, but a woman could only take so much.

She heard both men chuckle and realized her response had probably sounded more like a breathy plea than an answer. Cam kept his eyes on her, but spoke to Carl, "I'd say my lovely slave is curious about whether or not all of the things her friends from the Prairie Winds Club have told her are true." CeCe felt her spine straighten. *How did he know? Dagnabbit, sometimes he is annoying as all holy handball rackets. Living with someone this observant and insightful can be a real pain in my ass...ets—literally.*

"I'd have to agree, she seems quite interested. Even from here I can see the acceleration in the pulse beating at the base of her throat. Her respiration rate has increased and become much shallower as well. If I was going to bet, I'd say her pussy is as juicy as a ripe Georgia peach." The rich timbre of his voice only added to the lust she felt at Carl Phillips' words. She hoped she didn't go off like a rocket at his first touch. It would be mortifying to appear so untrained and embarrass her Master. CeCe wasn't a fool, she would hold back her release as she'd been told to, but she wasn't going to deny herself the opportunity to find out what all the ruckus was about, that would just be crazy.

CeCe felt like a deer caught in the headlights of two of the monster trucks she'd seen on the freeway on her way to the club. She became aware of each breath she took, could feel every beat of her heart and every time her pussy clenched with the need to be filled. The more aroused she became the more intense the ache in her core, she felt herself beginning to spin out of control and wondered how far they'd let her go before moving things along. *Get a grip, CeCe, they haven't even touched you yet, and you're about ready to come.* She realized their voices sounded distant and there were black spots dancing in her vision just as sharp pain lanced through her nipples. Gasping in a breath, she was shocked to realize she'd been so caught up in the moment she hadn't even remembered to breathe. *If their words can stop me from breathing, I'm not sure I'll survive it when they actually touch me?*

This time her Master's voice was razor sharp, "When you don't breathe, my love, your body doesn't focus very well, does it?" She was fairly sure it had been a rhetorical question, but she felt obligated to give her head a small shake anyway. "Above all things, I require that you take very good care of what belongs to me. Just as your safe word is there for your protection, it is in place for my peace of mind as well. I need to know that you will let me know *anytime* things are unsettling you to the point you forget to breathe, pet." She heard so many things in his words and tone that she wasn't sure she'd be able to sort them all out. CeCe knew he wasn't happy that she'd lost focus so completely, but she also felt as if he was misreading the situation. She wasn't sure he'd appreciate her assessment of the situation so she kept quiet.

"I think you may be overthinking things, Cam." Carl's voice sounded closer than it had a few minutes ago and she wondered if he'd actually moved or just leaned forward. "I think your lovely slave was so aroused by our observations she lost herself in the moment. From everything I've heard, she is a brilliant woman with an IQ that qualifies her for a Mensa membership, something neither of us will ever attain. But there are times words aren't the best way to grasp a concept. Perhaps showing her would be more effective." *Oh, he's smooth. Positively silky smooth. He's also full of shit because I'm betting his IQ is every bit as high as mine.*

Damn, if she got a chance she was so calling Tobi or Gracie. *Oh craptastic, I'm even starting to sound like Tobi.* They'd know the scoop on Carl Philips. Cam had said he was a part of the Prairie Winds team and that meant her friends would likely know all about him. Gracie would know because Jax was Cam's closest friend. And CeCe knew Jax wouldn't have sent the man here if he didn't trust him. She also knew Jax was the head of the club's security, but when she thought back, she realized Cam hadn't mentioned the club, he'd said "team" and she'd heard him use the term on occasion when referring to the men he'd worked with in the military. *I wonder—*

When she felt a hand cup the base of her skull her mind went completely blank. Good God Gertie, how had she managed to lose focus again so quickly? Both men were going to think she was a brat of the first order, or an idiot despite what Carl had just said. "I'm not sure what is causing all this distress, love, but I *do* think I know the solution." Looking up into his eyes, she was relieved to see a small curve at the corners of his mouth—just that hint of a smile put her at ease.

The truth of it was, CeCe had been struggling for months to keep her head above water. First she'd struggled with post-partum depression but had been foolish enough to keep it to herself for far too long. She'd also taken on far too many patients and that had cut so deeply into her time with Chloe, she often felt as if her daughter barely knew her. And having a full-time nanny living in their home would have been disruptive enough, but the woman was so vanilla that when Tobi had met her, she'd sworn her farts probably smelled like those cheap candles from Walmart. Not being able to relax in her own home had definitely taken a toll. She wasn't accustomed to wearing clothing at home because Cam had always insisted she be available for his visual as well as his physical pleasure. And not being able to play had robbed her of the opportunities to work off the stress and strain that had accumulated rapidly. There had been moments when she'd felt as if she was being drawn and quartered from being pulled in so many different directions.

When they'd spoken on the phone earlier, Cam had mentioned he planned to interview a new nanny before they left. She wondered if he'd still be able to now that their plans seemed to have been scrambled. She hoped she'd have a chance to at least observe the interview, after all, Chloe was her daughter too, even if the little imp had become a daddy's girl so quickly it was downright disgusting. She felt Cam's finger pressing between her brows and knew she had been frowning. "What was that thought?" There was an edge to his voice and she knew he surely must be losing patience with her little mental road trips.

"I was just thinking about Chloe, and how much she loves you. She is closer to you than she is to me and I don't really understand that." She felt her eyes fill with tears, but she blinked them back, willing them not to fall.

His eyes softened for just a moment before he shook his head, "That is only natural, I'm her father and she is so much like you already it's frightening. But it really is a discussion for another time." Placing his hands around her waist, he lifted her easily as he stood. Without even pausing, he managed to fold her knees as he placed her on top of his large desk. She'd barely registered her position when he stepped right up to the edge, looking down she found herself staring directly at his crotch. *Holy hat racks, it looks like it's trying to escape and that fabric can't hold it back for long.* "Pet?" Scrambling to keep herself propped up on the elbows while easing down the zipper of his trousers, she was careful not to damage the smooth head with the zipper's metal teeth. She'd known he wouldn't have bothered with boxers and she was suddenly grateful for his aversion to undergarments. Taking him in her hand, she marveled at how hot his skin felt beneath her fingers. When the musky scent of her Master wafted over her, she felt a rush of fluid fill her sex. A low chuckle from behind her reminded CeCe of Master Carl's presence. *Oh Lord, when had she started thinking of him as Master Carl? Don't get ahead of yourself, Cecelia. Just focus on bringing your Master pleasure and let him handle the rest.* That was the last thought that went through her head before she took him to the back of her throat and moaned around his flesh. Just holding him there sent pinpricks of electrical need sparkling through her, lighting her up from the inside. And then the whole world tilted on its axis when she felt Master Carl's fingers slide through her slick folds.

Chapter Five

CARL KNEW HE had probably startled CeCe, but Christ Almighty, there was only so much torture a man could take. He'd watched the interplay between Cam and his lovely sub until he'd started to worry he was going to make a fool of himself and come in his pants like an inexperienced teenage boy. The woman was beyond gorgeous. The pure passionate sensuality that surrounded her drew him in and he simply couldn't wait any longer to touch her. After the first slide of his fingers, he watched as she arched her back giving him a world-class view of her waxed pussy.

Leaning forward he pressed a soft kiss against each of her ass cheeks and smiled when she moaned as she pushed back for more. The vibration of the sound brought a curse from Cam, "Holy fuck that feels good, pet. Your mouth is like a hot, wet glove made of the finest silk." His head fell back and his groan let Carl know CeCe wasn't showing him a moment of mercy. Sliding his fingers leisurely through the warm honey coating her labia, Carl could feel the sensitive tissues swelling as her blood rushed into the fluttering petals. Lightening his touch to keep her dancing on the edge of release, he had to bite back his smile when he heard her growl of frustration. Leaning down once again, he bit her—not enough to break the skin, but enough for her to carry the mark the rest of the evening.

"Growling when you don't get what you want is considered bratty behavior at Prairie Winds, sweetness."

"And I swear I'd beat her lush ass if I had any desire whatsoever to pull out of her heavenly mouth." Carl grinned at the man's pained expression. And received a reproving look for a split second before his head fell back once again. "Christ, you'd better step up your game, Master Carl, because I'm not going to last much longer. Her tongue is playing a symphony on my cock."

Carl looked up and merely arched his brow. *Seriously? The man wants to challenge me? Well, I've learned a lot in the years since we last saw one another, my friend. Game on.* "Is that a fact? Well, in that case, Cecelia, I have a deal for you. You get your Master off before I get you off and you get to choose what we have for dinner, keeping in mind of course, I'll reserve the right to eat it off of your lovely bare breasts." He felt her sheath clench around his fingers in response and grinned. "And if I win, I'll choose. And just so you know, my fondness for hot fudge sundaes is almost legendary." This time she shuddered and moaned around her Master's cock as she redoubled her efforts. *Aha, so the little subbie has a competitive streak—good to know.*

Pulling the chair up with his feet, Carl lowered himself on to it, putting his face at the perfect height. He didn't waste a moment before leaning forward to cover her clit with his hungry mouth. The little nub had already been peeking out from beneath its hood begging for his attention. Flicking it with random speeds and pressure, he waited until he felt the first tremors quaking through her body and then he pushed two fingers into her depths. With the precision of the sniper he'd been, he drew upon all the experience he gleaned from years of practice with subs to press down directly on the spongy spot he knew would catapult her over the edge into a glittering abyss of pleasure. Her orgasm was so powerful he felt the flood of her release wash over his hand. Her scream took Cam over a split second later and Carl leaned down to press soft kisses against the sweet dimples at the top of her ass. "Perfect."

When Cam fell back into his chair, Carl felt CeCe shudder at the loss. He wrapped his arm under her and steadied her when her muscles started quaking from the isometric exertion of her muscles. "Whoa, baby. Let's get you up and settled a bit, shall we? I'm afraid we spun you up pretty fast, don't want you to drop on us." Carl had seen the effects of sub-drop and it had always reminded him of the adrenaline crash soldiers often experienced after a particularly challenging mission. It would be unsettling to her at the least and that wasn't the way he wanted her to remember their first session.

There was something special about CeCe and he wasn't sure exactly what it was yet, but he'd felt as if his soul had recognized her the moment she walked into the room. He and Peter had shared women for years, but he'd never felt the instant connection to any of those women that he'd felt with the sweet armful of curvy woman he held in his arms. When he turned to walk around the desk to place her in her Master's lap, he saw Cam wave him off with a pointed look to the sofa on the other side of the room. Shrugging, he turned and made his way over, sitting easily without letting her go. He settled back, relaxing as the cool leather upholstery soaked through the fabric of his shirt. Carl was grateful for the distraction of the flickering fire in the fireplace, hell, anything to take his mind off his aching erection.

When he shifted CeCe ever so slightly to relieve some of the pressure her soft curves were putting on his cock, he felt her giggle. "Well, I see you have recovered nicely, sweetness."

She looked up and he was struck by the depth of her dark eyes. He still couldn't tell if they were brown or a midnight blue, they reminded him of the Great Blue Hole in Belize—stunning in its depth and mystery. "I'm sorry, Master Carl, I wasn't trying to be disrespectful. Sometimes I'm just a little disconnected for a few minutes after I come that hard." Carl watched as she seemed to be choosing her words carefully before continuing, "I think you won. I don't supposed you'd be interested in hearing how much I was hoping for a nice bowl of room temperature soup for dinner, would you?" For the first few seconds Carl was too stunned by her words to determine if she was serious. But when she batted her eyes in that overly dramatic fashion that every little girl learns before potty training, he knew he was being played.

Carl knew his easygoing personality often kept people from taking him as seriously as they should—hell, he'd used it more times than he could count during enemy encounters. It was always a sweet moment to see the realization dawn in a target's eyes when they discovered his duplicity. Of course, it was always too late at that point, but he enjoyed that split second of awareness. But the mischief dancing in her eyes let him know she'd known exactly how far she could go to lighten the moment, and damned if she hadn't gotten it exactly right.

"Hmm, I'll take that information into consideration, but I have to tell you, lukewarm food of any kind isn't going to sound appealing to any soldier I know."

"No, I guess that would be true enough. Well, I guess I'll just have to let you handle it and know that you'll have my best interest at heart."

Cheeky sub.

CAM ORDERED A quick snack from the deli on the club's main floor and smiled at Carl's surprised look. "I found that members are often so rushed they don't get to eat dinner before coming in to play. Having food available helps them out, and working there gives subs a way help defray our hefty membership fees. It's turned out to be a win-win, and judging from Tobi's enthusiasm, I'd be surprised if Kent and Kyle don't do something similar in the future." Enthused was an understatement, Tobi West had literally been bouncing on the balls of her feet while he'd explained the details of Dark Desire's "Work to Play" program to the petite ball of fire married to his friends.

While they'd enjoyed the sandwiches, Cam realized the sexual tension between the three of them was still almost palpable. The moment Carl had put his hands on Cecelia the air around the three of them had nearly crackled with an attraction so powerful Cam swore the hair on his arms had stood up. He'd hoped there would be an attraction between his former friend and his wife, but he'd never expected the sizzling chemistry he'd felt during their earlier scene. Now the only problem was, he wasn't entirely sure how to manage the situation.

If he let it play out, without any input on his part, there was a good chance they'd all get scorched by the fireball that was sure to erupt. He'd seen these situations play out in the club several times over the years and the results had usually been disastrous. Without careful management, he worried when the smoke cleared there would be little left except ashes. But on the plus side, if he was careful, the potential for the future was phenomenal.

He didn't feel like he knew Carl well enough anymore to predict his behavior, but since circumstances had provided him the opportunity, Cam planned to exploit it. He's settled Carl and Cecelia in the small private room off his office. They'd be able to see and hear the interview. Before he'd left them, Cam had pressed a kiss against his lovely slave's forehead and reminded her to treat Master Carl as she would him. When Carl had raised a brow at him in question, he'd merely nodded and hoped his friend understood the implied message.

Cam was grateful Carl would be with Cecelia during the interview because he was certain the other man would understand exactly what was happening when he set off on the unusual path he planned to take with the questioning. He had been absolutely thrilled when he'd seen Lara's name on the candidate list the employment agency had provided. The woman he'd spoken with had been shocked at his choice, and he'd gotten the distinct impression she wasn't Lara's biggest fan—something he planned to check on during their upcoming chat.

Looking at the large bank of security monitors mounted on the wall of his office, Cam watched as Lara paced restlessly in the reception area. He hadn't left her waiting intentionally, but he had to admit having the beautiful sub a bit off-kilter would work to his advantage. Leaning back against his desk, he watched for a few minutes wondering how long it would take her to realize she was being studied by Fischer and Peter Weston.

LARA FELT LIKE she was going to pass out. She'd never been

this nervous before a job interview. *But you've never been interviewed for a day job by someone who's seen you naked, either. Oh God, now I'm talking to myself. This can't possibly end well. Master Cameron will probably drop a net over me and have me locked in a padded cell in the dungeon. Is there one down there?* She took a deep breath trying to banish all the crazy talk floating through her head.

She'd been on pins and needles since she'd received the call yesterday from the agency. And then when they'd called again this morning moving the interview up, she'd nearly panicked because she'd already been at the deli downstairs working. Sure, Master C had chosen her work uniform, so it probably wouldn't make any difference but, holy shit Sherlock, it seemed beyond weird to be interviewing in a bustier and fishnet stockings. Even if the outfit did cinch in her waist so she looked like some old time movie maven, and offer up her breasts in a way that was almost impossible to ignore, it wasn't anything even close to business attire. Damn it all, the skimpy cups barely covered her nipples, and there had been several occasions when she'd been so busy she hadn't even realized "the girls" were actually playing unencumbered on top of the lacey cups. And her skirt was so short her ass cheeks were visible—her very bare ass, since every Master in the club seemed to have some sort of strange hatred of undergarments. *Don't they know that walking around in public without anything covering your girly bits is breezy? Damn, this place is right at the water's edge and that fucking gulf wind blows right up where it isn't welcome.*

Lara knew she could change here at the club, but that would mean taking time to plan ahead, including packing a small bag and then remembering to bring it along. Sighing, she shook her head, it seemed like she was always running from one part-time job to the next like a chicken with her head cut off. It was a rare day when she had time to do any more than sprint into her tiny apartment, change clothes, and run back out the door. Half the time she didn't have what she needed with her—she'd actually started clipping notes to the outside of her purse for God's sake, how pathetic was that? Lord of all things logical, she needed a *keeper*.

Countless nanny and personal assistant positions had been open at the agency during the past year and she'd applied for each one and never even gotten an interview. The employment specialist she'd been assigned to hadn't bothered sugarcoating her explanation—Lara's personal appearance was the problem. Oh, it wasn't that she had a third eye in the middle of her forehead or that she was Martian green. No, this was an entirely different sort of prejudice. Expectant mothers took one look at her photo and moved her portfolio directly into the "never going to happen" stack.

At five foot five inches tall and one thirty, Lara had an hourglass shape that she worked hard to maintain, mostly because she really enjoyed food and found it easier to workout than give up any of her favorite treats. Her blond hair fell to her waist in soft waves that refused to be tamed despite all of her attempts to bring it under control. It unnerved her that strangers would often reach out and touch her hair—they always had the same glazed over expression as if it had just magically drawn them in—it was very odd if you asked her. Lara had been blessed with her mother's flaxen hair and blue eyes, but her dad's South American skin tone. She always looked as if she'd just returned from the Caribbean and her perpetual tan had boosted her confidence when she'd started playing at Dark

Desires. The other subs at the club had teasingly complained that she had been overly blessed by the "looks fairy". When she'd insisted it was a double-edged sword one night during a movie marathon, they'd peppered her with popcorn, boos, and hisses. It had ended up being an all-out food fight that had taken them over an hour to clean up at the end of the evening.

Her caseworker at the employment agency had referred to herself as a "voice of decency" when she'd warned Lara that her part-time position in "that den of inequity" would likely keep her from ever getting a *good* position. *For an old bat with such a hang up about sex, she sure uses the word position a lot.* Sighing, Lara felt as if she were caught between the proverbial rock and hard place. The friends she'd made at Dark Desires were the closest thing she had to family now that her parents were once again living on the other side of the globe. *You should be grateful they stayed stateside as long as they did.* Lara's missionary parents had honored their promise to her and stayed in Sealy until she'd completed high school, but they'd returned to the mission field the week after enrolling her in college. Giving up her job at the club's small eatery would mean giving up the only support system she had, it was an option she'd sworn she wouldn't consider, but recently she'd started to wonder if she wasn't painting herself further and further into a corner. And to be honest, she was getting awfully tired of eating macaroni and cheese.

When she'd gotten the call yesterday informing her she'd been chosen to interview for a position, she'd been too excited to ask who the employer was. Then this morning, the woman Lara thought of as Ms. Screech called to say the client wanted her to meet him at his office in two hours and then recited the club's address.

Lara had nearly dropped the phone when she'd been give Cameron Barnes' name as her contact. At first she'd been thrilled because she'd known her boss certainly wasn't going to look down on her because of her part-time job in his deli. But then she'd realized what she was wearing—and her excitement had waned considerably. And holy hellacious hairballs, being interviewed by someone who had seen you naked...and being flogged...and screaming the walls down when you came? *Nope, nothing intimidating about that!*

"Fuck me, I'm going to wear a hole in this rug if I don't stop. It'll be okay. It's just Master C. Nothing to worry over. Worry doesn't alter outcomes." Lara hadn't thought twice about speaking out loud, after living alone for so long she'd gotten used to giving herself pep talks. "It's not like a crazy lady who talks to herself is going to exactly stand out as odd in my neighborhood anyway. Nope, I'd have to step up my crazy-game several notches to even make the B-team on my block."

"Well, darlin', I'm definitely interested in fucking you, but we are going to be having a long chat about your neighborhood first." Lara froze. Her entire body *always* reacted to that voice. *No. Not now. Please.* She didn't know why in heaven's name her guardian angel was always on break when she managed to get herself into these pickles. Turning slowly, her eyes rested on a man that looked like Fischer, but was just a little older if she was to guess. He sounded just like Fischer, perhaps just a hint more subtly in his tone, but they were definitely cut from the same cloth. This man's hair was a bit darker, but his eyes were the same shade, somewhere between turquoise and green. She stood perfectly still, watching, waiting. Everything about him told her he was a Dom, but there was a gentleness about him that called to her. She'd often thought Fischer had the face of an angel, but this man looked like he'd seen too much—this man was a wounded angel. There was a sadness in his spirit she was sure most people didn't see because they probably failed to look beyond the gorgeous exterior. *Fuckidy-fuck. I so do not need this right now. I wait a year to get an interview. Then it turns out to be with my current boss, a man who knows more about me than my gynecologist, and then fate drops an angel in the room just in time to hear me chattering to myself like I've got bats in my belfry. Seems I've been promoted from hot mess to walking disaster. Go me!*

PETER HAD BEEN listening to his brother moon over a sub at Dark Desires for the better part of a year, but had yet to make the trip to the suburban Houston club to meet her for himself. He'd known Fischer was thrilled to learn they would be working together until the threat against Dr. Cecelia Barnes had been neutralized and suddenly Peter understood why. After arriving, he'd toured the club but by the time they'd finally made their way to the deli, Lara Emmons had already left. One of her co-workers explained she'd been called to Master C's office, so they'd both headed that way, taking different paths hoping one of them caught up with her before she reached her destination.

They hadn't planned to derail her—the opposite in fact. Fischer had insisted this would be a great opportunity for Peter to meet her, they'd catch up with her, with luck, and then wait until she was finished to take her out for a late lunch. Just before entering the ornately decorated reception area, Peter caught a glimpse of an agitated woman pacing the length of the room. He hadn't looked at Fischer—he hadn't been able to tear his gaze from the gorgeous woman pacing in front of him.

Adam, Peter, and Fischer Weston were all gifted empaths, but Fischer was by far the strongest, he'd mastered the skills as a small child. The youngest of the Weston boys had learned to speak telepathically to his brothers before he'd finished nursery school, and even though Peter and Adam had both worked hard to catch up, neither of them had ever been as gifted.

The two of them might have taken different paths on their way to the reception area, but they had arrived at almost the same moment. Peter didn't take his eyes off the luscious blonde staring at him with the clearest blue eyes he'd ever seen, but he sent out his thoughts and hoped like hell his brother caught them. *'If this is the woman you've been raving about, my sincere apologies for not coming here months ago.'* Fischer's snort of laughter let him know his brother had indeed caught the message, it also alerted Lara to Fischer's presence. When her eyes darted to his brother, Peter saw them dilate. *Perfect.*

Chapter Six

LARA WAS CAUGHT in the gaze of the stranger whose blunt admission that he was interested in fucking her sent a surge of desire through her that nearly stole her breath. She could feel moisture pooling in her sex and all he'd done was speak to her. The sound of a man's soft laughter to her right broke the spell and when she turned, she looked into eyes the same shade of green, but this time it was Fischer.

Fischer Weston might have the face of an angel, but Lara wasn't fooled. Fischer was a wolf in sheep's clothing. She'd rarely seen him give a woman so much as a second glance, and she'd heard murmurs among the uncollared subs that he was gay. Lara had disagreed, but wisely kept her opinion to herself. She'd learned early on to keep herself out of the way of the merciless grinding stone of the club's rumor mill because anything that could pulverize someone else to dust could certainly do the same to her. She'd been the victim of bullying when she'd attended public school for the first time. From that point on, Lara had sworn off gossip and negativity. When her parents returned to the United States so she could attend high school, Lara might not have dressed in the latest clothing, or known about everything "trending" among her classmates, but she'd traveled the world with her missionary parents, and she'd known how to make friends. Learning to read people was a survival skill for a kid that moved every three to six months, and she'd mastered the skill early on.

Lara had seen the way Fischer looked at her, at first he'd seemed confused, as if there was something different about her that he couldn't figure out. But just a few weeks after she'd started at Dark Desires his gaze had turned molten. There had been times when she'd been playing with another Dom and she had known he was nearby watching because she'd literally been able to feel his gaze on her.

Fischer ate at the deli almost every time she worked in the small eatery and he always engaged her in conversation. But despite the fact she could see the desire in his eyes, he'd never asked her to play. She had finally stopped hoping for anything more and just enjoyed his friendship, assuming that was all there would ever be. Since he'd never given her any indication of what was missing between them, she'd eventually stopped trying to figure it out.

"Fischer, what are you doing here?" Lara heard the note of edge in her voice and grimaced when he simply raised a brow at her. "I'm sorry. I wasn't trying to be rude. I'm just really nervous right now." *And being in the same room with two hot Doms is not the solution.* She hadn't realized she was wringing her hands together until he glanced down where she had them clasped together in front of her. He didn't react or respond, he just continued studying her. His scrutiny was doing nothing to allay the tension she'd been feeling but she managed to stand still despite the fact her body had kicked into fight-or-flight mode and the scales were tipping precarious toward the flight side of things.

By the time Fischer pushed his shoulder away from the doorframe he'd been leaning against to take a step toward her, Lara was wound so tight she instinctively took a step back without even thinking. When her back came up against a warm chest, she gasped and would have taken a quick step to the side but a long, muscular arm banded around her just below her breasts. "Stop," the deep voice of the man behind her washed over her in a warm wave of desire that made her realize her body had responded to his command before her mind had even registered the word, the realization thrilled her and terrified her in equal parts. "We aren't going to hurt you, precious." When he leaned down and pressed his lips against the tender pulse point below her ear, Lara knew she wouldn't be able to hide her racing pulse from him and shuddered in response.

FISCHER WATCHED EVERY breath Lara took, each beat of her pulse as it pounded at the base of her neck. The woman fascinated him, even at a distance where the thoughts of other people were usually muffled, Fischer felt drawn to her. The first time he'd seen her, she'd been standing at the reception desk dressed in a floral sundress she probably mistakenly thought hid her lush curves. Even though she hadn't spoken the words, her disappointment when she'd seen the membership fee had been written all over her pretty face. When she had simply nodded and turned to leave, he'd stepped forward and asked if she would be interested in the work program the owner was implementing. Fischer thought back on the wide-eyed look she'd given him, she'd confessed later that she'd wondered if he had been joking or hitting on her. That afternoon it had taken her so long to reply that he had begun to think she wasn't going to. And then he had almost missed her hesitant nod because it had been so small.

There hadn't been a single day since he'd met Lara that Fischer hadn't thanked God above for that chance meeting. Well, except for the day she'd filled the entire club with smoke when she'd put cupcakes in the deli's open oven. The look on her face when the local firefighters burst into the room had been worth the price of admission. But the crowning moment had been listening as she explained to a bewildered fire department captain why she'd thought a broiler oven was a reasonable option for baking. Since Fischer had been privy to the man's thoughts, Fischer had known the captain hadn't been sure whether to arrest or cuddle her.

Cam had lectured her for over an hour on the importance of clearing any future cooking "inspirations" with her supervisor or anyone else with a "lick of common sense—perhaps some third grader". The stricken look on her face had quickly turned mutinous, and the glare she'd given her boss had earned her a punishment Fischer doubted she'd yet forgotten. Since they'd been forced to close the club on a Friday night, the club's owner had given any Dom who had already scheduled a scene a chance to participate in her punishment. Master C had secured Lara in the stocks on the main stage, bared her lovely ass to the entire room and stood by as the offended Doms each gave her a couple of solid swats with an oak paddle. Fischer had finally interceded, reminding Master C that she'd been trying to do something nice for *his* birthday and hadn't intentionally caused the mayhem that ensued. He still called her cupcake on occasion, and always enjoyed the sweet flush that burned her cheeks each and every time he used the nickname.

Peter's soft chuckle told Fisher he'd picked up the

memory that had been replaying in his mind. "Cupcake?"

Lara groaned in embarrassment as her face went crimson. "How did you know?" Then she'd moved her gaze to his, "You told your brother that story? I can't believe you would do that, and I know he's your brother because, well—just because. And please, please, please don't do this to me right now. I have a really important interview with Master C and I just can't cope with your rejection right now." Before he'd even sorted through her words, Peter's voice snarled in his mind. *'Rejection? What the fuck? Is she kidding? She thinks you don't want her?'*

Before Fischer could answer, Cameron Barnes stepped into the room. As usual, the man didn't miss anything, his gaze had barely moved between the three of them before he'd smiled and nodded his head. "Come along, Lara, I don't want these two flustering you before we've had a chance to talk."

Fischer wanted to growl in frustration as his boss led the very misinformed sub from the room. When he turned back to his brother, he saw Peter looked just as annoyed as he felt. "She doesn't know? You haven't told her what you were waiting for?" When Peter didn't even try to hide his frustration, Fischer knew how truly pissed off he was. "What the fuck were you waiting for? You told me you were sure she was the one, why didn't you make sure she didn't get away?" When Fischer didn't answer immediately, Peter began pacing, much the same as Lara had been doing when they'd found her. "You can't hear her can you? That's how you knew she was the one, but it also kept you from knowing she feels as though you have rejected her. Does that about cover it?"

This time Fischer found his voice, "Yeah. I remembered what Granny said—you know, about knowing we'd found *the one* when our gifts didn't work well on her. But to be honest, I wasn't sure at first because, well—because she really did seem too good to be true. And I wasn't sure what to do with a woman I couldn't read." He ran a frustrated hand through his hair, "Hell, I still don't know what to do with her, and I've known her for almost a year." For the first time in his life Fischer understood what life must be like for other men, how utterly frustrating it was to have no idea what was going on in a woman's mind. And because he usually *did know,* he'd felt like he had suddenly been tossed blindfolded into a room full of obstacles just before someone set the damned house on fire.

HOLY MOTHER OF all things sacred, what the hell had that been about? Fischer was hard enough for Lara to deal with, his intensity had always made her feel like an inexperienced teenager, but his brother was lethal in a whole new way. Struggling to keep up with Master C as his long legs ate up the distance down the hall, she decided to put the two men out of her mind so she could concentrate on the interview. As they entered his office, Lara had the strangest sensation of being watched, but when she let her eyes move quickly around the room she noted they appeared to be alone. When she returned her gaze to Master C, she saw that he was leaning back against the front of his desk, hands curled over the front edge of the glass top and his ankles crossed casually as he studied her.

Lara had worked at the club long enough to know better than to fidget under the watchful gaze of a Dom, but damn it, Master C was intimidating and she felt like every muscle in her body was clenched tightly. She'd read about the fight-or-flight instinct and suddenly those words took on a whole new meaning. The man's office was such a contrast to the rest of the club she couldn't help but look around, she tried to appear casually interested, but assumed he knew she was just trying to distract herself.

The utilitarian décor might have appeared stark to some, but she'd been raised in all varieties of primitive conditions while traveling the world with her parents, so she appreciated the simplicity of the décor. The only piece in the room that appeared to be starkly out of place was the antique clock on the fireplace mantle. The ornately decorated black and gold timepiece was ticking so loudly it made her think of the beating heart in Edgar Allan Poe's story, *The Tell Tale Heart*. She felt an involuntary shiver race up her spine just thinking about the story that had given her more than its share of nightmares when she'd been a kid. When she shuddered at the memory, he smiled, "What is it about my grandmother's clock that made you shudder, sweetness?"

She grimaced because she certainly didn't want to insult his grandmother or her clock, its place of honor in his office told her how important the piece was to him. And damn it, she knew better than react so overtly, handing a Dom any additional information was always dangerous because they'd use it ruthlessly. But there wouldn't be any escape from answering so she'd just as well get it over with. "Well, Sir, the sound reminded me of a story I read as a kid that scared the bejeezus out of me. I had nightmares for a long time about that darned story."

He laughed out loud and Lara realized that it was a sound she hadn't heard very often. Her expression must have given her away, but this time he merely raised a brow at her. "Sorry, it's just that I realized I don't hear you laugh that often and it was nice to hear. I've heard that Dr. Barnes is having a bit of a security challenge, and well, I just hope it is all cleared up soon and that you'll be able to find more reasons to laugh."

PEOPLE RARELY SURPRISED Cam. In fact, they rarely ever had. Hell, for the most part he found people in general to be boringly predictable. He'd admit that he'd been a bit surprised at the instant connection he'd seen between Carl and Cecelia, but Lara Emmons has just shocked him to his toes. The insightful sub had pointed out a fact he himself had only recently figured out, he'd become so focused on making Dark Desires successful he'd forgotten what was truly important in his life. He'd been toying with making some huge changes in his life and her words added to his commitment to fully explore all of the options.

First things first though, he had an interview to conduct. If the plans that had been slowly solidifying in his mind worked out, little Chloe wouldn't need a nanny here in Houston much longer. He wasn't going to worry about that, because unless he was reading the situation entirely wrong, Lara wouldn't be available much longer anyway. He'd seen the writing on the wall when he'd walked into the reception area. The Weston brothers were more than a little interested in the beautiful woman that had been standing nervously between them. Cam knew the two brothers hoped to find a woman to share, but their ability to hear the thoughts of others made long-term relationships difficult at best. One night after a particularly difficult evening at the club, he and Fischer had shared a bottle of A.

H. Hirsch Reserve and his club manager had shared his grandmother's advice on how to identify the woman meant for them. Judging by Fischer and Peter's intense attention earlier, Cam was guessing Lara was that woman. The trick was going to be keeping her on staff long enough to put his dream into action.

When she had first come to Dark Desires, Cam hadn't been convinced she knew what she was getting into. A conservative young woman who had been raised by evangelical missionaries in some of the world's most remote locations seemed like an unlikely candidate for Dark Desires. It had quickly become obvious the woman studied everything—with the exception of cooking—as if she planned to master each topic she encountered. He'd reviewed the resume the agency had forwarded and when he'd compared it to the one he had on file for her he'd been surprised at all she'd accomplished in just one year. Deciding the best way to find out what her long-term goals were was to simply ask, he smiled and queried, "You have been very busy this past year. I've read the information the employment agency provided and compared it to your file from a year ago, and I have to tell you I'm impressed." He was pleased to see pink staining her cheeks, *love a sub whose built-in lie detector is right out there for all to see.* "What are your plans for the future? You're racking up an impressive number of degrees, but they seem to be lateral."

Lara had obtained several bachelor degrees as well as finished her Masters in two of those disciplines and he was curious about why she seemed to be scattering her education in different directions rather than focusing on one path until she'd finished her doctorate. She pulled her bottom lip between her teeth, chewing on it as she thought. He didn't get the impression she planned to lie, just that she was trying to figure out how to explain.

"Well, no disrespect intended, but after talking with several of the doctoral candidates, I realized they were so smothered in paperwork most of them had forgotten why they had ever even been interested in the topic. The whole process appeared to be simply a question of which of them would be able to navigate the paper maze they were caught in." Since they were both still standing he could see her shuffle her feet adorably, hell, she'd even drawn a couple of small circles with the toe of her raggedy sneakers. Now that he considered that, he thought back on the rare occasions he'd seen her in street clothes and remembered everything she'd worn had been threadbare. Jesus, had he really been that negligent? Had he simply assumed she was out and about running errands in her worst clothing when she always seemed meticulous in her personal appearance at the club? He made a mental note to add a clothing allowance to the salary package he planned to offer her.

Cam nodded once to let her know he'd understood her explanation, even though he still wasn't sure what drove her to continue attending classes. He'd never particularly liked school, he was more a hands on learner, and one of the reasons the military had worked out perfectly for him. Then years later—once he'd gone private it had just been about continuing to do what he'd done so well, but for a lot more money. He'd invested his earnings well and wouldn't ever need to worry about money, hell, his various accounts around the world meant his great-grandchildren likely wouldn't ever need to worry about funds either.

"Tell me about the woman you have been working with at the employment agency." He had deliberately refrained from phrasing his inquiry as a question. He'd learned years ago that submissives responded much more openly to orders for information than to questions. He was sure some psychobabble specialist had probably spent millions of taxpayer dollars studying exactly *why* it was true, but Cam didn't give a shit about that. He believed in dealing with what was true and then figuring out a way to make that reality work for him, the why of it didn't matter.

By the time Lara finished recounting the many challenges she'd faced while dealing with the judgmental wench at the agency he was seeing red. He made a mental note to speak to Fischer, they needed to make sure none of their other part-time employees were facing similar prejudices in the job market. He also wanted Fischer to be aware the woman he was interested in hadn't bothered to disclose the trouble she'd been having with the woman. Even though she didn't "belong" to Fischer or his brother yet, her fierce streak of independence was something they would probably need to watch for if they managed to convince her to take them both on. The owner of the agency was a long time club member and after the note Cam had just tapped into his phone to the man, he was certain the woman who had treated Lara so badly would be looking for another job in short order.

Refocusing his attention on the beauty standing in front of him, Cam smiled at the newfound confidence that seemed to have filled her. He'd seen her spine straighten and knew she hoped to shift the interview back to focus on the position she was applying for. Smiling to himself, he planned to make her a lot more uncomfortable very soon.

Chapter Seven

CARL WATCHED THROUGH the two-way mirror as Cam began questioning the young woman the agency had sent for the nanny position. "She is wearing a Dark Desires uniform. Why?" He hadn't meant for his question to sound so abrupt, hell, he'd been retired from the SEAL teams long enough he should be able to remember not everyone communicates in such an abbreviated way. When he glanced at CeCe, he saw her studying him carefully. It was if he was a puzzle to solve and even though her scrutiny shouldn't have mattered, it did. He didn't ask, just raised a brow at her in question. When she flushed in embarrassment at being caught staring he knew she'd been lost in thought and now he was even more curious.

She finally managed to speak, her words were halting as if she wasn't sure she had permission to speak, he and Cam clearly had different styles of dominance. "Lara works in the club's deli. She is one of the subs who is allowed to work at the club part-time in order to offset their membership fee."

Carl would never be comfortable with the level of intensity Cam had maintained in his relationship with CeCe and the sooner she learned to relax in his presence the happier they would both be. "CeCe, while Cam and I are both Doms, we have different views of how that should look in private. When you and I are alone, I'll expect you to be respectful, but I want you to speak freely. Did you have a boyfriend in college?" Even though her eyes were still a bit wary, she nodded slowly. "Okay. Absent other instructions when we are alone, I want you to treat me the way you would treat a boyfriend in that context until we know one another better. Once we get comfortable, we'll rewrite the parameters. Understood?"

"Yes, Sir." Carl chuckled at her automatic response and the pink that flooded her cheeks when she realized what she'd done. *Good God she is beautiful, no wonder Cam is enraptured with her.* And there was no question why his friend was completely over the moon with his lovely wife. Carl hadn't seen Cam in years, but there were things about a person that never changed, and the genuine emotion in Cameron's eyes was easy to see.

"Well, sweetness, I think perhaps this is something we'll just agree to work on. The only time you'll find I am absolutely unwilling to compromise will be when safety is the issue, and that applies to you and Chloe. At those times I'll demand your immediate compliance." Her heart shaped face paled, but she nodded, so he continued, "I'll expect your obedience during play, but I'll enjoy punishing you as well." He was relieved when the flush that began over her heart spread all the way to her cheeks and the muscles in her shoulders appeared to relax.

"Now, while we watch the rest of this interview, I want you to become familiar with my touch. Your Master has given me carte blanche, but I think we'll both feel better if you have a chance to acclimate a bit first." With those words, Carl pulled her in front of him, her bare back against his chest so she faced the large window. He wrapped his arms loosely around her and began caressing her breasts with one hand while he kept the other splayed over her lower abdomen. The only thing keeping them from being completely skin-to-skin was the thin fabric of his shirt, and he was beginning to resent its presence. When he felt her begin to relax against him, he began pinching and pulling her nipples, alternating his attention between the two and pulling them into tight peaks. "Your breasts are very sensitive, aren't they? Were they sensitive before you had Chloe?"

"Yes, Sir." Her head was pressed against his breastbone and the airy sound of her voice went directly to his cock. The woman was every man's wet dream fantasy come to life in Carl's opinion—brilliant, beautiful, and a natural submissive. She wasn't overly thin, thank God, but she was more slender now than she'd appeared in the photos he'd been given. Later he would ask Cam if she'd lost weight recently because if he had to make a guess, he'd say she'd been struggling before the threats became an issue. He certainly didn't want her to lose any more of her sweet curves, he'd never cared to hold a women who felt like a stick. And despite the fact he didn't really know her, Carl noticed she also seemed much paler than her photos in the file the Wests had provided. When he'd casually checked her palms, the light color of the lines told him she wasn't eating right, and he'd be willing to bet her work schedule had prevented her from spending any time working out as well. Even though he'd technically retired from the SEALs, his work for the new contract teams the Wests had put together meant he was still training regularly so he'd be able to put together a workout for the two of them. She'd probably curse him in the beginning, but once she noticed how much more energy she had, he'd be willing to bet her complaints died quickly.

"Perfect. You and I are going to be spending a lot of

time together, and I'm going to have my hands on you a lot. I love the way your skin feel beneath my fingers. Your small shivers and sweet moans are a siren's call to a Dom." Pressing his mouth over the pulse point below her ear, he could feel the pounding of her heart as it beat rapidly. *Aha, so the sweet sub's calm demeanor is a well-practiced ruse, huh? Let's see how long she can maintain it?*

Just as he slid his hand between her legs, he heard Cam asking Lara if her hard limit list was up to date. And when he asked the young woman if she was still opposed to playing with married men, CeCe's entire body went rigid. Carl didn't stop touching her when he spoke, "Darlin', stop and think. Why would he ask her that question?" She'd started trembling so hard he was surprised her teeth weren't rattling. The woman wasn't thinking logically, this was an entirely emotional response. Pulling his fingers from her slick pussy, he turned her away from the window. Swiping his wet fingers over his jeans, Carl then used his fingers to tilt her face up to his own. Hell, if he'd thought she was pale before, her skin was almost translucent now. The vacant look in her eyes told him that her mind was racing and not in the right direction. "Cecelia, look at me." When her dark eyes didn't zero in as he'd hoped, he snapped, "Right now, CeCe. I want you to really look at me. Focus and use that razor sharp mind of yours." She nodded as if the words had finally gotten through, so he continued, "I haven't seen or talked to Cam in two and half decades and even I know exactly what he's up to, and you will too if you'll just stop and think."

He was relieved when he saw the glaze recede from her eyes and turned her back to the window just as Lara explained to her boss in crystal clear terms that she didn't— nor would she ever play with a married man. She also told him that she'd really been interested in the job, but she couldn't keep it if it involved fooling around with him. Carl was barely able to hold back his laughter when the little spitfire Cam had been interviewing said, "I'll have you know you have an amazing wife and beautiful daughter, and I hope to hell you don't do anything to fuck that up." When he saw her eyes go wide, Carl knew she realized what she'd just said to her boss, a man who also happened to be a Master in the club where she was a submissive. She pressed her lips together so tight they were actually turning blue and the color was a sharp contrast to the pale color her face had suddenly turned.

Cam merely watched her for several seconds before he smiled. "Don't worry, Lara, that was exactly the response I was hoping for. Your loyalty to my wife and daughter are precisely what I'm interested in. And as for your sassy response, that sort of conviction to personal ideals is a trait I'd demand rather than punish in this particular instance." Lara finally took a breath and a little bit of color reappeared in her pale cheeks.

"The job is yours if you want it. You'll begin drawing the nanny's salary as soon as you read and sign the paperwork," he said, nodding toward the small stack of papers at the corner of his desk. "I'll also see to it that your things are moved into our home immediately." When the young woman's eyes widened, Cam shook his head, "Stop and think, Lara. You will have a nice suite of rooms that is larger than your current apartment, and you will be far safer there. We have had a recent threat against my wife, Carl Phillips and I are taking her away for a few days while things are resolved. It would be almost impossible for anyone to mistake you and Cecelia for one another, so you'll be safe in our home, and I'll arrange for you to be escorted anytime you leave the penthouse. I checked your address, sweetness, and you are living in a very dangerous neighborhood, it's time to get out of there before your luck runs out."

Carl was having trouble holding back his amusement at Lara's expression and looking at CeCe's expression in the window's reflection, he could see she was facing a similar challenge. Cam hadn't lost his ability to steamroll people. Hell, it was more likely the life he'd been living since they'd known one another would have exacerbated the trait.

Carl knew all too well how being a part of the Teams had intensified several of his own personality quirks. His tendency to drive like a Formula One driver had certainly gotten worse, as had his habit of questioning everyone's motives—including his own. Even now there was a huge question hanging over his head, but he was going to push it aside because he intended to take full advantage of the free reign he'd been given with CeCe. Turning her so she was facing him, Carl smoothed her hair back and waited several seconds for her to settle before speaking, "Never doubt his love for you, sweetness."

"Why haven't you two seen each other in so long? What happened?" Her questioned shocked him and from the look on her face, she seemed equally surprised she'd let the words slip free. He didn't respond at first because he'd been too stunned to formulate an acceptable answer. Since he and Cam hadn't discussed how to address this particular issue, he wouldn't answer the question she had every right to ask. Well, he wouldn't answer right now, so his only option was to keep her distracted.

"That's a story for another time, sweetness. Right now, I'm going to exercise my right to enjoy that sweet mouth of yours." To her credit she didn't argue, she simply dropped to her knees and waited for his instructions. He was grateful for her patience because he wasn't planning to let anyone else unzip his pants for fear his cock might make a leap toward the temptation and get caught in the zipper's brass teeth, hell, just thinking about *that* scared him. "Rest your hands on my thighs, baby, and keep your eyes on mine." He didn't want her worrying about keeping her balance, he'd much rather she focused all of her attention on their mutual pleasure. The depth of CeCe's submission showed in her expressions and he didn't intend to miss anything. He would also know exactly where her head was if he could see her dark eyes.

"We'll start slow, because you aren't familiar with my style of dominance yet. But, baby, I have to tell you, it isn't going to stay that way for long." He took himself in hand and pressed the tip forward smearing the pearly drops of pre-cum over her lush lips, reveling in the shiny gloss it painted over her bow shaped mouth. *Damn, the woman's mouth was made for a man's pleasure.* "Open for me, baby." The warm silk of her mouth wrapped around his length and his knees nearly buckled. "Holy fucking hell." *The woman has no gag reflex? None at all?* He'd never had a sub take him clear to the back of her throat on the first pass. Sweet baby Jesus, if she had swallowed before he'd pulled back he would have probably come right then. *Fuck me the woman's mouth is deadly.*

"Your mouth feels so good, I'm not sure if it's heaven sent or devil blessed. But it's fucking amazing either way." He let her set the pace for the first few strokes, but when he saw her eyes glaze over with lust he knew it was time to grab the reins or she was going to take them both over far too quickly. Wrapping his hands in her hair, he gave it a quick tug when she moaned and closed her eyes, "Eyes on mine, sweetness. Don't disobey me. I'm looking forward to paddling your sweet ass, but I'd much prefer the kind of spanking that brings you pleasure to anything resembling punishment." The truth was he didn't know her well enough to punish her. And he could find far better ways for them to spend the next few minutes.

Carl heard Cam enter the room, but he was sure CeCe had not. His former friend was standing to the side watching and even though Carl hadn't looked at him directly, he could feel the heat of his gaze. *Perhaps he is remembering the last time we were together.* Before his mind could stray too far in that direction, he returned his attention on the woman kneeling in front of him. Her eyes weren't leaving his, but they were so unfocused he was certain she wasn't really seeing anything. "Are you wet, baby? If I slide my fingers through the soft petals of your pussy would I find them soaked with your honey?"

When CeCe nodded her head frantically, Carl placed his hands along the sides of her face taking away her peripheral vision. Stepping back he didn't move his hands as he said, "Stand up." When she scrambled to her feet, he turned her so her ass and bare pussy would be front and center in Cam's view. "Spread your feet apart and bend at the waist, baby, let's kick this up a notch." He saw her puzzled expression but she followed his instructions without hesitation. There wasn't any way for her to keep her eyes on his now, and he hated the fact he wouldn't see her surprise when Cam pushed into her from behind. But she took him back in her mouth tracing the large vein running the entire length of the back of his cock with her tongue and his eyes nearly rolled to the back. Now that he thought it over, it probably didn't matter if he couldn't see her face since his head was lolling backward and his eyes closed in pleasure of their own volition. He had already been hard enough to pound railroad spikes into the sunbaked Texas prairie and now he was worried the whole thing might burst into flames as well.

His friend didn't waste a moment freeing himself from his trousers and pushing in deep. The force of his thrust pushed CeCe forward so Carl's cock hit the back of her throat. Her soft gasp of surprise vibrated around him, and almost sent him barreling over the edge. "I am pleased to see you and Master Carl are getting along so well, pet." Carl felt her mouth tighten around him and on his next thrust she swallowed, the massaging muscles of her throat made him growl with pleasure.

"Baby, you are killing me with that mouth of yours. Holy fuck!" Carl was battling to stay on his feet, hell, his knees were already shaking and he hadn't even come yet. Looking up at Cam, Carl was shocked to see the man's focus on him rather than the woman he was thrusting himself into. The lust shining in his friend's eyes and his own body's response answered many of the questions Carl had struggled with for years. Why *this* man? Carl had *never* reacted to a man before he'd met Cameron Barnes, nor had he reacted to any man since they parted that fateful night so many years ago. But the feeling that slammed into him felt like being hit in the chest with a sledgehammer, and for a few seconds he didn't even remember to breathe. How would the two of them be able to resist the temptation to take one another again when they were going to be spending all of their time together? And how would Cam ever explain everything to his sweet wife, because it was obvious he hadn't told her about him?

Realizing he'd lost focus, Carl ran his hands through CeCe's hair and praised her wickedly skilled mouth,

"Sweetness, you are going to undo me. Your mouth is so hot and your tongue is touching all the right places. Tighten your lips a bit and suck hard as I pull back." When she did exactly as he asked, Carl's head fell back as he groaned in satisfaction. *Better get her there quickly or she's going to send you sailing and you're going to leave her standing on the shore.*

Leaning forward, Carl cupped her breasts in his hands, lifting the weight of them with a gentle squeeze before zeroing in on her tightly drawn nipples. Rolling them between his fingers, he smiled at her low moan, "Aha, baby likes to have her nipples pinched, I see. I'll bet your Master has all sorts of beautiful ornamentation for these lovely buds. Personally, I'm particularly fond of pierceless nipple bead rings. Lots of stimulation without putting holes in your lovely breasts." Carl wasn't a fan of needles and firmly believed you shouldn't subject a sub to them. If a submissive was looking for that kind of play, then he wasn't the right Dominant for her. But he certainly wasn't above taking advantage of a sub's piercings if she already had them, there wasn't much of anything prettier than a woman's jeweled breasts.

When Carl had first been introduced to the lifestyle of BDSM, he'd approached it like a typical cryptologist—he'd researched it relentlessly and taken each element apart with meticulous detail until he understood exactly how it worked and how each piece fit with the next. As a cryptology expert, he'd learned that almost everything was a puzzle in one form or another, and if you studied it carefully enough—the pattern and therefore the solution would be revealed. The bottom line for success in the lifestyle turned out to be finding a submissive whose needs aligned perfectly with his own. Just as with most precisely machined puzzles, the pieces had to fit together perfectly or nothing worked.

Cam was glaring at Carl and finally growled, "Get there. Right. Fucking. Now." Carl raised his brow in response. *Maybe he isn't having any more luck holding out against her pussy than I'm having with her mouth.*

"Okay, sweetness, let's take a trip over the moon, shall we? Come now, baby." Carl was sure CeCe had started coming before he'd even taken a breath. His cock was pushed all the way to the back of her throat and her muffled scream sent rippling vibrations up the entire length of his cock. He felt the electric charge of his release burn a path up and back down his spine then settle in his balls, turning his cum molten. The shockwaves of pleasure that radiated through his entire body splintered out making his fingers and toes tingle as he pumped the hot spurts of his seed down CeCe's throat. Carl couldn't remember the last time he'd come so hard that he had actually seen sparkles of white light dancing behind his eyelids.

He'd heard Cam's shout and when Carl's eyes were finally able to focus, he realized CeCe was still bent at the waist with his fingers twisted in her hair. *Fuck me, I'm an ass.* He gently unwrapped the silken strands of her glossy dark hair from his fingers and pulled her slowly back upright. Wrapping his arms around her, he hugged her against his chest while Cam put himself back together and then walked through a door that Carl assumed led to a washroom. When he returned, Cam knelt behind CeCe and Carl heard his soft murmurs urging her to part her legs. Carl chuckled when he heard her sleepy voice claiming she couldn't move anything and maybe he could check in with her again sometime next week. Carl lifted her feet from the floor while Cam opened her legs. Once she'd been cleaned and dried, Cam wrapped her in a soft blanket and carried his sweet bundle to the bed.

Carl excused himself to clean up. Returning, he found CeCe sleeping peacefully on the bed and the door to Cam's office open. Walking through, Carl saw Cameron sitting on the leather sofa with his legs stretched out over the low table in front of him swirling the amber liquid in the glass he held in his hand. There was an empty highball glass setting next to the bottle of Glenfiddich. *Should have known he'd have expensive taste in whiskey.* Carl made himself comfortable before pouring a generous amount of the wonderfully smooth Scotch, he let it warm his throat as it slid south. Hoping the liquor would work its magic before the conversation started, Carl leaned back against the sofa and tossed back the rest of his drink.

Chapter Eight

"TO ANSWER THE question I've seen in your eyes a dozen times since you got here—no, I haven't told her." Cam's voice held apprehension, but Carl wasn't sure what had him so keyed up. Was he worried his lovely slave would bolt? Maybe he was worried Carl was going to spill the beans and wreak havoc in his marriage. *Christ, this thing may well be a clusterfuck before it ever even has a chance to start.*

Deciding it was best to walk on the side of caution, Carl simply asked, "And?" It had been twenty-five years, but Carl could still feel the bond between himself and Cam as if it were almost tangible. The connection between them wasn't as soul stealing as it had been twenty-five years ago, but it was still strong enough Carl had easily heard the enormous unspoken "but" at the end of Cam's statement.

"Truthfully, it has just never come up." Even though Cam wasn't facing him directly, his profile was a study in frustration and tension. Hell, everything in Cam's body language attested to his struggle to put his feelings into words. Cam's unsettled feeling was probably unfamiliar territory for a man who'd made a career of being unflappable and always in control. Hell, Carl was all too familiar with the fact Cam's life would have depended on his ability to push emotion back to the point the man often wondered if he'd ever be capable of really *feeling* again.

Carl had been lucky, the last rescue mission he'd done

as a Navy SEAL had been for a young woman who had meant the world to a couple of his friends. Jen Keating, now Jen McCall since she'd married Sam and Sage McCall, was a handful of the first order. Her sass, the fire in her eyes, and her ability to call out anyone around her had reawakened Carl's hibernating soul. Watching his friends with Jen had made him wonder if there might be a woman out there with enough love to look past everything he'd seen and done. When he'd joined the Prairie Winds team, he'd gotten to know the other women his friends had married. Meeting Jen, Tobi, and Gracie had proven to him that his heart was still capable of loving.

There was no doubt about Cam's love for CeCe, it was written all over his face. Carl understood how hard it must have been to conceal the truth from her. Anytime you hide a large part of yourself from the one person you are supposed to trust the most, it divides your attention and saps your energy. He didn't know Cameron Barnes well enough anymore to anticipate what he might be planning, so he'd just wait the man out. One thing was certain, Cam's lifestyle and his club would have provided him plenty of opportunities to replicate what they'd shared, so if CeCe didn't know about their relationship, Carl had to wonder if Cam had abstained—just as he had. *Interesting.*

They sat at opposite ends of the same sofa, drinking glasses of Cam's expensive Scotch until the bottle was empty. *Thank God it hadn't been a full bottle or we'd both be out cold before one of us gave in and spoke.* Cam finally set his empty glass on the table and leaned forward, resting his elbows on his knees. He took a deep breath and Carl could practically feel the man's frustration fading away. "I've had a million and one opportunities to tell her. But I managed to find an excuse each and every time. It isn't that she is judgmental, but she's always seen me in a very specific role and I never wanted to risk damaging her view. God knows I'm terrified of losing her."

When he finally shifted in his seat, turning to look at Carl, for the first time he saw fear in the man's eyes. "Cecelia is a strong woman professionally. She is an excellent mother even though she doesn't get to spend nearly as much time with Chloe as she would like to. She is a loyal friend and an understanding partner. Her submission to me is the greatest gift I've ever been given. But there is a layer of vulnerability that runs so deep even I only see brief glimpses of it on rare occasions."

"And you think she'd feel like she had never really been enough for you if she found out? Is that it?" Carl had spoken softly because he didn't want to wake CeCe, but he hadn't tried to keep the disbelief out of his voice either. "You aren't giving her much credit if you ask me." When he saw Cam winch, he added, "Funny, I wouldn't have ever taken you for a coward. But hell, what do I know— I've never told anyone either." Although he didn't have a woman in his life to tell, he'd never told anyone.

"Told anyone what?" CeCe's soft voice sounded from the doorway. *Hell.* Carl wanted to groan out loud. How had two former Special Forces operatives both failed to see the very beautiful and very naked woman standing across the room from them? She didn't move, nor did she ask anything else—she just waited patiently for an answer. Cam recovered first and simply held out his hand to her. Her feet seemed to move before her mind had a chance to register the gesture—she was obviously a very well trained submissive. Even though Carl wasn't a stickler for every nuance of the lifestyle, he was always impressed when he met subs who were so in tune with their Dom that their trained responses appeared almost effortless.

As CeCe sat on Cam's lap, Carl noticed her skin seemed to have a light blue tinge, he reached over and wrapped his hand around one of her small feet and shook his head, "Christ, baby, your feet are like ice. Hang on a minute." He walked quickly into the room where they'd left her sleeping earlier, pulled the blanket from the bed, and returned. Once she'd been wrapped up and resettled on Cam's lap, he sat back down next to them. Looking up, he found her dark eyes staring at him, clearly not intending to let her earlier question be forgotten.

CAM LOOKED AT the woman sitting on his lap as she turned her gaze to him and hoped like hell it wasn't the last time he saw such love and devotion reflected in her dark eyes. "Carl was talking about the fact neither of us have told anyone why we haven't seen one another in so long." He glanced at the empty bottle of Glenfiddich and wished like hell he'd brought out a bigger bottle. "The last time we saw each other, things didn't go well." Realizing his words would probably be misunderstood, Cam clarified, "The problem wasn't between the two of us, but the school officials who were none too happy with us." His chuckle sounded hollow, even to his own ears and he let it die quickly.

"I don't think I'm following this. Why would the school officials being angry with you keep you apart for so long?" Cam leaned forward and kissed Cecelia's cheek, grateful color was returning to her sweet face.

"Pet, Carl and I were very close at that time in our lives. We both came from families that were extremely wealthy, wealthy enough to ship off the wild sons they didn't have the time or desire to manage. Sons who the school officials promised to tame." Cam thought back on how betrayed he'd felt when his family had first sent him to St. Andrew's. The school's reputation for strict discipline had been well earned. He'd endured beatings with wooden paddles so severe he hadn't been able to sit comfortably for weeks. When those punishments failed to turn him into the robot the dean had promised to produce, the Headmaster and his lackeys stepped up their game with caning.

The night they'd had to take him to the infirmary for stitches had been the final straw as far as his friend, Carl, had been concerned. By then, he and Carl Phillips had become extremely close, although their relationship had yet to take that final step. When Carl snuck into the infirmary to see him, he'd been horrified at what he'd found. It was the only time Cam ever remembered seeing Carl Phillips cry. His friend had never shed a tear during any of the punishments he'd endured, but that night Carl sat beside Cam's bed and cried for his friend.

Cam had tried unsuccessfully to convince his friend that getting himself into trouble wasn't going to help, but Carl had been beyond the point where he would listen to reason. Cam still remembered the wild look in Carl's eyes as he'd vowed he would "take care of it". And take care of it he had. The Headmaster was beaten so badly late that night he'd resigned and left the school the next morning. The two men who had pressed their obese bodies against Cam's as they handcuffed him to the large rings set in the rock walls of the subbasement had suffered similar fates. All three men had been gone before noon the next day. None had identified their attacker, convinced of the promises of further retribution if they talked to anyone about what had happened.

Carl had never admitted being responsible, but there had never been any doubt in Cam's mind who had evened the score for him. He'd spent the last two weeks of that school term in the infirmary battling a series of infections. Most of the time he'd been too delirious with fever to complete the schoolwork his teachers had delivered each afternoon, and the nurses always marveled that despite the fact he was so ill, Cam's work had always been completed by the next morning. Most days Cameron hadn't even remembered Carl sneaking into his room and working all night to complete both sets of homework, but his friend's handwriting had been unmistakable. He would have been forced to repeat his freshman year if it hadn't been for Carl Phillips' unwavering friendship.

Realizing he'd been lost in his memories, Cam smiled, "I'm sorry, pet, I was thinking back to our freshman year. I was even more stubborn then if you can imagine that." Her smile warmed his heart as he went on to tell her some of the antics he had been involved in and how those had been handled by the staff at St. Andrew's. Between Cam and Carl, they'd remembered so many stories he'd found himself laughing right along with her when she'd shaken her head and said she hoped their daughter didn't inherit her father's lack of respect for authority. But she'd shed several tears when they'd told her about the caning that had landed him in the school's infirmary.

"We didn't see each other during that first summer, but when we returned to school in September our friendship was even stronger than it had been when we'd parted the previous June," Cameron paused because this was the point of the story when everything changed. One touch had changed both of their lives forever.

When Cam felt like his throat was closing, Carl continued the story. "CeCe, things had already started to change at the end of our freshman year. Cam doesn't remember a lot from those last two weeks because the fever he battled often made him so delirious he barely knew his own name. He's forgotten so much of that time, but it really never mattered because after we came back as sophomores our relationship changed very quickly."

Cameron watched as understanding dawned in Cecelia's dark eyes. He hadn't even known he was holding his breath until he realized her expression was one of compassion, not condemnation. He saw her reach for Carl's hand at the same time she pressed a soft kiss to his cheek. "You two had a physical relationship, didn't you? Is that what you have been so worried about telling me?" When Cam nodded, she shook her head indicating his worry had been unnecessary. "I don't know whether to tell you how hot the idea is or to pout because you thought I'd condemn you."

Carl leaned his head back and laughed out loud before pulling her hand up to press kisses against her knuckles. "You are absolutely enchanting, CeCe. It's no wonder Tobi and Gracie speak so highly of you." She blushed a deep crimson as he pulled her forward, kissing her chastely on the lips. "Your reaction doesn't particularly surprise me though, hell, I don't know you well enough to know *what* to expect, but you intrigue me. I'll admit I also feel like a giant cement block has been lifted from my chest, and I'm sure Cam is going to say the same thing once he finds his tongue again." Carl's words seemed to kick Cam's brain back into gear and he pulled his beautiful wife in for a plundering kiss that was meant as a promise as much as it was an expression of gratitude. Her unconditional love and acceptance were gifts straight from heaven, and he promised himself he'd make sure she knew just how grateful he was.

Cam didn't pull back from her lips until his brain was screaming for oxygen. Once he'd finally caught his breath, he said, "You never cease to amaze me, pet. Your capacity for love and understanding are most likely going to get you nominated for sainthood one day." When she laughed he nodded once before setting her on her feet. "I need to make a couple of phone calls and then we need to head to the airport. We aren't flying commercial, but that doesn't mean I want to keep the pilot waiting. Your luggage is already onboard the jet, love, so all you need to do is head back to the locker room and dress. Carl will accompany you." When she looked surprised, he smiled, "Let's not forget we're dealing with a security issue and you will not be out of sight until we're convinced you are no longer in danger. I agree that Dark Desires should be a safe haven for you, but I'm not willing to bet your life on it." He knew she had changed in the smaller staff lounge rather than the larger locker room members used, but that still didn't mean she would be safe from harm if someone really was intent on hurting her.

As soon as he was alone, Cam braced his hands along the edge of his desk, and tried to calm his racing heart. She knew. She knew the truth and she hadn't called him a freak or a pervert like the school officials and his parents had done. His parents had allowed him to stay in their home long enough for him to join the military and ship out. The night before he left for boot camp was the last time he'd slept under their roof. In fact, he hadn't seen either of them personally in years. They'd sent their regrets when he and Cecelia had gotten married, and they had conveniently been out of the country when Chloe was born.

Picking up the phone, Cam called Fischer asking him to make the appropriate arrangements to move Lara into the penthouse and gave the man a head's up about the harassment she'd endured at the employment agency. He could have sworn he'd heard the man growl. Fischer assured him *they* would make sure she was moved in immediately *and* that he'd address the issue of transparency with her. Cam wasn't surprised to hear that his second in command and his brother would both be accompanying her. His team had deliberately put the word out that he and Cecelia would be enjoying an extended vacation and their daughter was in the care of family members. Anyone doing even a minimal amount of research would discover Cam's favorite escape, and that was exactly what they were hoping for.

Cam had known Fischer was interested in the young woman he'd hired, but he'd said he needed to wait for his brother to arrive before acting on it. One night after the club closed, he and Fischer had shared a few drinks and Cam had confessed his envy of Fischer's gift. His friend had rotated his bottle of Utopia in slow circles making a design in the condensation that reminded Cam of a game he'd had as a kid, but he couldn't remember the name.

"Spirograph," Fischer's tone hadn't been mocking, but it was easy to read his expression. "See? It isn't just about *hearing* what people are thinking, often the biggest challenge is not completing their sentences for them or answering the questions floating around in their minds. And the quickest way to scare off a woman is to let her know you can hear her thoughts." Cam had been stunned as the truth of Fischer's words sank in. He had never considered how difficult life might be when you could hear what people were thinking, he'd only seen the advantages.

After that night, he'd had a sincere appreciation for how challenging working at Dark Desires had to have been for the man he'd grown to respect and considered more of a friend than an employee.

Remembering Fischer explaining his grandmother's prediction that the right woman's thoughts wouldn't be an open door, Cam couldn't help but wonder if Lara was the one. Now that he thought back, Fischer had always taken a keen interest in the beautiful young sub. He'd warned off several Doms who had expressed an interest in her even though he'd never topped her himself that Cam was aware of. The fact Fischer had waited for Peter, and they were both going to be spending time with her, made Cam smile. *I hope it works out, even if it costs me a nanny. Fischer deserves the happiness I've found with Cecelia.*

His second call was to his contact on the island. Juan answered on the first ring and Cam had to hold back his chuckle. He'd discovered that one of the unseen perks of having money was that people tended to answer your phone calls—God he hated voice mail and swore it had been invented by Satan himself. *Fuck me, I'm starting to sound like my dad.* His father's hatred for all things electronic had earned the old man many eye rolls from those around him—behind his back of course because crossing the man who signed the checks wasn't ever smart. *Makes me wonder how many times I've been on the receiving end of those same looks of impatience.*

Chapter Nine

"JUAN, IS EVERYTHING in order?" No need for preliminaries and he needed to wrap this up before Cecelia and Carl returned.

"Señor Barnes, good to hear from you. We will have everything ready to show Dr. Barnes, no worries. The sisters are very excited to meet her, they have been researching on the internet—they have all gotten smartphones now, so they are always researching everything. Mother Mary and baby Jesus, they are making Father Joseph crazy with this."

"Juan, while I appreciate Father Joseph's problem, that isn't why I called. I just needed to know if you would have everything ready for Cecelia's tour. I want her to see the potential, but she needs to know how much you need her as well." Cam understood what he was requesting would require a delicate balancing act, and Juan really didn't know his wife well even though they had met a few times, but he hoped the man could pull this off.

The casual tone was gone from the man's tone when he replied, "Señor Barnes, we need your wife's skills as a surgeon more than I can begin to tell you. There are three young children at the clinic as we speak who might one day be able to walk if they had the proper treatment. But our doctor is old, he does what he can but he doesn't have your wife's expertise," Juan paused but Cam knew he wasn't finished, so he simply waited, "One of those children is my niece, Mr. Barnes. I assure you I will do everything I can to convince your wife that her skills are needed. We will be ready, sir. Our children—they are our future. I promise you we will be ready."

He heard Juan take a calming breath before he added, "And Mr. Barnes, this is a small island, everyone knows there are men working on your home." Juan paused and Cam could practically feel the local leader searching for the right words. "Your wife will be safe here, sir. No strangers will be on the island that I do not know about. We look out for our own."

Cam felt as if the final weight had been lifted from his chest, knowing the people on the island would be watching out for Cecelia was a huge relief. In his experience, small communities were often the safest simply because strangers stood out so quickly, so knowing the locals would be on the alert would amp up their security exponentially. "Thank you, Juan. I can't tell you how pleased I am. We'll see you in three days." Disconnecting the call, Cam looked around his office and smiled. His plan had taken a big hit when the threats to his family started, but he was starting to wonder if the Universe hadn't thrown him that curve in order to bring Carl back into his life. In the end it didn't matter, his first responsibility was his family. Their physical safety and comfort, as well as their emotional well-being, were all that mattered.

CECE LOOKED AT Cam as they entered the elevator in what had to be the most opulent looking building she'd ever seen. She hadn't recognized the name on the front, but considering her husband's former life, it probably wouldn't have mattered if she had. One of the things she'd learned was when it came to Cameron's former life, very little was what it first seemed. She couldn't help but wonder who had provided them a place to stay for the first couple of days. The man who'd met them at the door hadn't given any indication who had arranged things, he'd merely asked for their identification. When he was finally convinced they were in fact the contacts he was supposed to meet, he'd escorted them to the elevator and upstairs.

Looking out of the glass backed elevator, CeCe wondered how secure it was even if the view was spectacular. "Dr. Barnes, I can practically hear that brilliant mind of yours whirling with questions. But first of all, let me explain the windows which are showcasing one of the most beautiful views in the city are in fact bulletproof one-way mirrors. The glass is specially treated to hide heat signatures as well. In the case of an attempted security breach, this elevator automatically descends into a sub-basement safe room. The only place on earth you *might* be safer would be Fort Knox, but I wouldn't bet on that."

She didn't even ask how he'd known she was thinking about the glass, he was obviously some sort of well-trained security expert and God knew that was certainly not her area of expertise. She simply smiled and nodded, "Thank you. I was curious and I appreciate your explanation." As they exited the elevator, she noticed Cam and Carl worked together effortlessly to position themselves at her sides just as they had done since the three of them had left Dark Desires together hours earlier. She hadn't realized how tired she was until she glanced at her watch.

"Pet, I know you are exhausted, but you really need to eat something before you rest." Cam was looking at her, his concern for her well-being was one of the things she loved the most about their lifestyle. CeCe knew his words had been spoken with love, but they were still a command so she simply nodded.

Since she didn't know the man leading them down the hall she was careful to keep her whispered, "Yes, Master," quiet enough only the two men at her sides could have heard her. As soon as they entered the condo, the smell of food washed over her and her stomach growled in response. "Oh my God in heaven, is that lasagna I smell? And garlic bread?" This time all three men laughed. "Because if it is, somebody is racking up points like a champ." When she rounded the corner and saw Tobi West across the room, she screamed and ran straight into her friend's open arms. CeCe wasn't sure why she was crying—whether it was fatigue or hunger, but she was thrilled to see her friend nonetheless.

"Hey, why the tears, girlfriend? Oh hell, you don't think I cooked this do you? Because I assure you I did not, and I can prove it." CeCe pulled back and looked at Tobi in question. "Seriously, did you see fire trucks outside?" CeCe had forgotten about all the harrowing tales she'd heard about Tobi's culinary attempts, and just as quickly her tears were replaced by a bout of giggles.

Behind her she heard Kyle West's voice, "It always amazes me how quickly women can switch gears, it is truly remarkable. And I heard your curse word, kitten. That will cost you five later." CeCe didn't know Kyle well, but the gleam of mischief in his eye told her Tobi had nothing to fear from his promised punishment. Turning to CeCe, he smiled warmly, "We're glad you are here. Your Master felt you might enjoy having a companion and since none of the well-behaved submissives were available, I brought Tobi."

His grin told her he was teasing his spirited wife and CeCe couldn't hold back her laugh.

"Hey! Don't laugh at him, it only encourages him to be snarly." When he growled something to her about additional punishment, she grinned, "Promises, promises…all the time with the promises." When he swatted her soundly on her curvy ass, she yelped and then turned into his arms and stood on her tiptoes to press a kiss against his lips. The love between them was easy to see and CeCe wondered if their ménage relationship suffered when Tobi traveled with just one of her husbands. Tobi turned back to her and grinned, "Come on, we need to feed you so you can rest a bit before we go shopping."

CeCe knew she had to look as confused as she felt when Kyle laughed, "Our lovely wife isn't always good about explaining herself very well, my brother and I tease her about speaking in shorthand. And it's one of the many reasons it takes two of us to keep up with her. The security team didn't want to have you out on the busy streets in broad daylight—that would draw more attention than we are interested in at this point." *At this point? What does that mean? Are they planning to draw attention at some point in the future?* Cecelia's mind was racing with questions when she suddenly realized Kyle had stopped speaking.

Looking around she realized she was now sitting on a sofa with Tobi at her side. Her friend's arm was wrapped around her shoulders and Carl was kneeling in front of her holding her hands in his. She felt shudders moving through her and had no idea what had happened. "Sweetness, look at me." When she focused on his face she hated the concern she saw reflected in his blue eyes. "You back with us now?" She nodded and he pulled her to her feet, "Let's get you fed and rested before we finish this conversation."

Walking toward a large table that was already set, he whispered against her ear, "Remember that you don't have to go out later if you don't want to, Cam and I will be perfectly happy to keep you *entertained* here."

CeCe appreciated his attempt to break the ice—damn her little "checking out" moment had sure thrown a bucket of ice water on her reunion with her friend. But to her credit, Tobi seemed concerned, but not overly worried. "Come on, girlfriend, I worked my fingers to the bone on this meal." When several of the men surrounding them laughed, Tobi's mock outrage helped CeCe relax after the tension that had pervaded the group moments earlier. "What? Do you know how many different restaurants I had to call to find just what you all wanted—*and* one that would deliver since none of you wanted to give up your keys? I was definitely having a George Jetson moment, I'm telling you for sure." CeCe burst out laughing—God she loved Tobi. The woman's ability to lighten a moment was something to behold and their mutual friend, Gracie, swore it had saved them both more times than she could count.

Cam and Carl seated themselves on either side of her and quickly filled her plate with more food than she could possibly eat. Glancing around, she asked, "Where is Kent? Did he stay home with the babies?" She hadn't seen him and just assumed he was back at Prairie Winds with their young twins.

"Right here, darlin'. You didn't think I'd miss seeing you, did you?" Kent's deep voice and southern drawl made CeCe smile. While she liked both of the West brothers, Kent was more easy going and she'd found him easier to talk to. He leaned down and pressed a kiss to the top of her head before moving around to sit beside Tobi. Grinning at his impertinent wife, he asked, "I thought I heard something about punishment a minute ago—you get yourself in hot water while I was gone, sweetness?"

"Not really, Kyle's hearing is failing and he wants to take that out on my backside. Completely uncalled for, I need to double check the details of that cruel and unusual punishment amendment."

Kyle growled, "I'll show you cruel and unusual punishment, kitten. Just keep digging, darling." Everyone burst into laughter and CeCe felt the last of the tension drain from her as they shared a wonderful meal filled with many of her favorite foods. Stories were bantered around and she had completely forgotten why they were all together until they sat back after dessert and she saw Cam nod to Kyle.

"CeCe, we're all working on finding whoever is responsible for the threats to your safety. Bringing us in lets Cam and Carl focus on protecting you. The rest of the Prairie Winds team will help, but we'll also be doing the track-downs, perimeters, etc." He paused and CeCe knew he was waiting for her to acknowledge her understanding so she nodded. Evidently he was satisfied because he continued, "No one wanted you to feel like a prisoner here. After all, it is supposed to be a well-deserved and long overdue vacation for you. But we also needed to control as many variables as we could, so, we've persuaded a few of mom's and Tobi's favorite boutiques to open up for you at midnight. We'll let you shop while it's easier to protect you. Kent and I have learned from experience that allowing Tobi loose on the city isn't wise, she tends to forget where she is and becomes quite lax about her own safety. That gets her in to a significant amount of trouble that I doubt you'd enjoy." *No shit! My Master is a real stickler about that sort of thing.*

Looking sheepishly over at Cam, she noticed his half smile. "Well, that does seem to be a sticking point for my Master as well. I'd prefer not to get myself into trouble the first day of vacation." *Can you say understatement?* The last time her Master had been *concerned* that she wasn't taking her safety seriously, she had found herself over the spanking bench in the club for a paddling that had forced her to stand through meetings the whole next week. And for the first time she had been grateful that surgeons stood during their often-long hours in the operating theaters.

CARL LEANED BACK against the chair in the corner of the large bedroom he was sharing with the Barnes' and looked over at Cam, "We need to figure this out before we go any further, you know. It isn't fair to CeCe. She shouldn't be left swinging in the breeze on this." Rubbing his hand over his face in a move sure to give away his frustration, he looked up at the only man he'd ever let touch him and wondered what he was thinking.

"Could you love her?" Cam's blunt question shocked Carl. Of all the things he'd envisioned the man saying, this hadn't even been on the horizon.

"What?"

"Could you love Cecelia the way she deserves to be loved?" Carl watched Cam as he seemed to struggle with voicing whatever was playing through his mind. "To be honest, the idea of adding another person to what we have isn't new, well, it isn't new to me. I've seen the sparkle in her eyes as she talked about things Tobi and Gracie have shared with her. I'm not sure what we have is enough for her now that she's seen what a ménage relationship looks like." Carl was shocked at his friend's words, from everything he'd read about Cameron and Cecelia Barnes, their relationship was the envy of envy of everyone who knew them. Hearing that Cam saw a weakness in the life he'd built surprised him.

"Does she know you thought there was something missing in your marriage?" It didn't really matter how Cam answered the question, because the truth was, Carl *was* drawn to CeCe in a way he hadn't ever been to another woman. Even reading her file as he'd flown to Houston had intrigued him. *Could* he love her? Absolutely. *Would* he? Only time would tell. Was he interested in seeing where things went between them—all three of them? Yes.

"That isn't a fair question, because I didn't feel as if something was missing or lacking, I merely wondered if what we had couldn't be *enhanced*. Surely you have heard Kent and Kyle talk about the advantages of a ménage." When Carl simply nodded, Cam continued, "So often the strongest women are the most adept at concealing the feelings her Dom most needs to know, but with two men seeing to a sub's needs it is much more difficult for her to conceal anything. Also, consider the differences in Kent and Kyle's personalities—they aren't so different from the way you and I are in temperament, they each meet very specific needs for Tobi. There are other benefits as well—obviously, but I'm most interested in providing Cecelia with the emotional intimacy I'm not able to give her." Carl knew that admission hadn't been easy for Cam, hell, it wouldn't have been easy for him to admit either.

Carl wasn't as worried about being able to connect with CeCe as he was re-connecting with Cam. He'd always carefully avoided anything resembling the relationship he'd had with Cameron Barnes. Maybe avoided was the wrong word because he'd never even been tempted. And heaven only knew how many nights he'd passed the time under the stars of some godforsaken hellhole of a country whose name most people couldn't even pronounce wondering why Cameron Barnes had been the only man to draw him in. Was his disinterest due to the disastrous way things had gone down that night? But the more likely explanation was that he'd simply never found another man with whom he'd been so physically and emotionally drawn to. The connection he'd felt back then had been so strong it had been impossible to resist—the two of them had been like atomic magnets, and their relationship had filled a part of Carl's soul he hadn't even realized was vacant. Over the years he'd convinced himself that time in his life had been a unique mix of circumstances and the attraction was an aberration he had outgrown. He'd been so certain that if he were to meet Cam again, the attraction would have disappeared, or at least faded. He'd been wrong.

Taking a deep breath, Carl spoke, "The short answer is yes—CeCe is definitely a woman I could love, but I think you already knew that."

Cam studied him for long minutes, not saying anything, just swirling his Glenfiddich around in his glass before lifting it and draining the last of the expensive Scotch in one swallow. *Jesus, Joseph, and Mary, even watching his throat muscles flex is arousing. What the hell?* "Is it true? What you told Cecelia about not being with any other man since we were together—is that true?" Carl wasn't thrilled that Cam was questioning his honesty, but there was a thread of vulnerability in his voice that kept him from lashing out at the perceived insult.

"Yeah, it's true. I don't lie. I may tell you something isn't any of your fucking business, but I won't lie to her or to you. Ever." His response had likely been gruffer than necessary, but he wanted to make a point. Honesty was something he had always prided himself on—hell, it was what had sent everything into a tailspin that night at St. Andrew's. If he'd just gone along with Cam's version of the story, he would have walked away virtually unscathed, but he hadn't been able to do it.

"Good enough. And just for the record, I wouldn't have expected anything less than your complete candor." Cam paused as he poured more Scotch into his glass before speaking again, asking the obvious question, "Why?"

And there it was—the same question he'd just been considering and had asked himself thousands of times over the years. Why was it only this man? Hell, he'd never been remotely attracted to any other man, but from the moment he'd walked into Cam's office, Carl had been almost hobbled by a lust-fueled erection. He couldn't even count the times he'd had to remind himself he was here on assignment. CeCe's safety had to remain his number one priority, his chief responsibility was to the lovely woman sleeping peacefully just a few feet away, but they needed to clear the air as well.

"I don't know." *And not for lack of consideration, I assure you.*

Chapter Ten

THE SOFT SOUND of rustling sheets drew both Carl's and Cam's attention to the lush curves of the woman laying nearby. CeCe had pushed the dark Egyptian cotton sheets off just enough to reveal the gentle curves of her toned back and the top half of her sweetly rounded ass. God the woman was almost glowing in the moonlight that was streaming through the window. Her pale skin was a contrast to her dark hair and Carl made a mental note to make sure they had plenty of sunblock when they got to the island. He was going to enjoy applying the lotion to every exposed inch of her and he was certain all of those delicious inches would be exposed most of the time.

"She is beautiful, isn't she?" Cam's expression was as soft as Carl had ever seen it, but he had the impression his friend was apprehensive about his relationship with CeCe. "I was in the front entrance the first night she walked into Dark Desires. I don't believe in coincidence. Things happen for a reason, but I have no idea why the Universe thought me deserving of such an amazing gift." Carl saw the same haunted look in Cam's eyes that he'd seen in his own and each of teammates over the years—the vacancy that spoke of the things they'd seen and done. "But like any former operative, I'm an opportunist. I wasn't about to let her walk back out the door with her application packet without talking to her. And I damned well wasn't letting any of the newbie Doms that had suddenly found their way to the reception area get their hands on her."

Carl didn't speak, he simply waited as Cam seemed lost in the memory of that night. "I know you have probably heard about love at first sight and like me, you probably scoffed at the idea. Don't. It's real. From the moment I looked up and saw her standing in front of me, she was mine. I fell in love with her as soon as our eyes met and I swear to you I felt lightning race up my arm when she shook my hand." Carl wanted to laugh at Cam's pained expression, "Christ, I sound like a fucking Hallmark card, but I'm telling you it's true. I kept her here that night for hours, helped her fill out her packet, she'd already done a physical so all that remained was the background check. I didn't play with her that night, but it took every ounce of restraint I possessed. Hell, Fischer would have had a stroke if I hadn't followed my own rules." Cam's laugh was strained and Carl nodded in understanding. Kyle and Kent hadn't let either he or Peter play until their background checks were done and they'd been teammates and friends for years. Not that a background check on a Navy SEAL is going to tell you jack shit, but it looks good on paper if anybody wants to question it.

"There is something about the threats you received that bothers me. They are worded more to gain *your* attention than to really show intention to harm CeCe or Chloe." It was an understatement and they both knew it. The threats were seriously lame and definitely focused on Cameron rather than the intended "victims". Carl's best guess was that it was some woman Cam had failed to "notice" and she would eventually show herself—but he certainly wasn't willing to bet CeCe's or Chloe's life on it.

"Jax and Micah drew the same conclusion, but I haven't seen that yet. I'm not sure I am able to look at it objectively, I'm terrified of losing either Cecelia or Chloe, but my instincts tell me Cecelia is more of a target, which leads credence to your observation." Carl respected Cam's admission that he was unable to be objective in his analysis, many Dominant men wouldn't admit to being fallible. But Cameron Barnes had been an agent for a lot of years, and survival in that world depended on acknowledging your own weaknesses—so you could compensate for them because it often meant the difference between life and death. Cam's willingness to request the help of a seasoned team of security specialists was testament to how seriously he was taking the threats.

"The envelope just showed up on your desk? And your security feeds don't show any activity in the area during that time?" Carl knew what was in the report, but after seeing all the surveillance equipment at Dark Desires, he had trouble imagining anyone eluding all the cameras and making their way into and out of the owner's inner sanctum without drawing attention.

"Yes. And no. Well, the security feeds for the entire building show plenty of *activity* for those minutes, but not anything particularly useful." Cam snorted in frustration, "We have a particularly interesting five minute segment of *Debbie Does Dallas* spliced in to the same time frame for every camera in the building. So whoever we're dealing with knows what they are doing and just how long it would take to make their way to my office and get out."

"Did you walk it through?" Timing would be an important element. Whoever tapped into the security feeds wouldn't have wanted to leave the porn film on any longer than necessary.

"Yes. And from the front door, it takes three minutes

and from the side entrance that is used by staff, it would take four." Carl was betting his friend had a theory, so he'd wait to hear the rest of what Cam had to say before offering his own opinion. "Personally, I'd put my money on the side entrance. The front entrance is caught in a sweep from the street cameras which are not connected to our system, and the side entrance is hidden by landscaping as a part of the design."

"I think maybe you should have Micah re-run the background checks on each of your employees. He still has a lot of military contacts, their systems are more difficult to skirt. Do you by chance remember anyone whose record appeared almost *too clean?*" Everyone knew that a created background was usually squeaky-clean and therefore highly suspect, but for some reason those didn't always flag, so they often eluded investigators. Cam simply nodded and began typing into his phone. When he had finished, Carl met his gaze and asked, "What about you? Anyone since we were in school?" He hated how needy the question sounded, but he deserved an answer—it was only fair.

Cam's eyes dilated as their eyes stayed focused on each other, the lust Carl saw in Cam's eyes felt like a blast of heat blowing through the room. "No." Carl hadn't known how much the answer meant to him until he felt his body let out the breath he'd been holding. Cameron's answer had almost been too forceful, so Carl just continued to watch him closely. Carl knew there had been rumors around the school that he wasn't the only one Cam had topped, but he'd never taken any of the stories seriously. The two of them had spent so much time together, Carl wasn't sure when his friend would have had time to see anyone else. But over the years, Carl had learned most relationships don't remain exclusive forever. Hell, almost every couple he'd ever known had dealt with the subject of infidelity, and it didn't matter if they were in a traditional marriage, ménage, or same sex relationship.

Cam had just opened his mouth to speak when they heard Cecelia gasp as if someone had frightened her followed immediately by a blood-curdling scream Carl was sure would bring the entire team bursting into the room. Before he and Cam made it to her side the door was flung open and men with guns drawn ran in tracking the entire room before settling on the three of them.

It wasn't a surprise to anyone when the team's newest member, Mitch Ames, was the first to speak, "Well damn, nobody to shoot? What am I supposed to do with all this adrenaline now?" He grinned at Kyle, "Boss, this job may not work out if'n I don't ever get to shoot anybody."

Carl saw the mortified look on CeCe's face ease when Kent's snort of laughter broke the ice, "I better get back to Tobi, she was spittin' mad as a wet kitten when I locked her in the closet in our room. Unless of course Mitch here wants some excitement after all."

"Nope. I may be an adrenaline junkie, but my mama didn't raise me to be suicidal or stupid. Wet kittens are lots more dangerous than gators." Mitch Ames could play that poor southern boy routine until the end of time and Carl wouldn't buy it. The man might have been raised in the bayou, but his mama and daddy were anything but poor, they owned one of the largest oil companies in the south and God only knew how many offshore rigs they owned as well. Mitch had joined the Army after a night of drinking during which he'd gambled away his car and his girlfriend had shoved him out of the cab too close to a recruiter's office. His family's money could have gotten him out of the commitment he had signed, but that wasn't Mitch. The man had excelled, becoming a Ranger then a Green Beret.

He was the Prairie Winds team's newest member.

"Coward."

"Damn skippy." The exchange hadn't taken long, but Carl could feel CeCe's muscles relaxing under his hand and he was grateful for Mitch's insight. The man was going to be a huge asset to the team, his easy manner might appear effortless, but Carl knew better. Mitch had chosen to leave the Special Forces because he'd been disillusioned by all the restrictions and limitations he felt prevented his team from being as effective as they could have been. From what Carl heard, Mitch's team had gotten to a young female hostage too late because they'd been held up by administrative red tape. Kyle told the team that Mitch's re-enlistment paperwork was shredded and returned to his commanding officer within hours of his team's return to Fort Bragg.

The room emptied and Carl could practically feel CeCe's adrenaline crash coming on. Hoping to get some answers before that happened, he turned so he was facing both CeCe and Cam. "Want to talk about it?" He hoped to vanquish whatever demons had brought her awake screaming as if the hounds of hell were chasing her. To his credit, Cam just held her hand offering his support, but not giving her an out to answering the question.

The small wrinkles that formed between her eyes let him know she wasn't entirely convinced talking about it was the way to go, and he had to bite back his smile. She really was cute as hell when she was frustrated. He could almost hear the gears of her mind speed shifting. "Well, I was on the beach and a man walked up and stood over me. The sun and shadows kept me from seeing his face, but there was something familiar about him. He just said he needed to 'clear the path' whatever that means. And then he raised the gun he was holding and I started screaming."

CeCe was trembling so hard Carl wondered if her teeth

were rattling. Cam pulled her into his arms and just held her for long minutes. Carl mouthed *man* and Cam simply raised a brow in question. When she seemed to have stopped shaking, Carl watched as Cam opened his arms and sat back. "Are you sure it was a man? Have you had this dream before?"

"Yes and no. It's so strange because I so rarely remember dreaming. I know they say everyone does, but I just never remember doing it. And, it just seemed so real…please don't tell my sister—you know how she gets."

At Carl's questioning look, Cameron answered, "Cecelia's sister, Camille, is quite superstitious, and fascinated by all things *extraordinary*. Fischer tends to avoid her as much as one can avoid a sister-in-law simply because she asks him more questions than an annoying three-year-old does. She badgers him until he wants to throttle her. Adam swears she is far worse than their children ever were."

Carl leaned his head back and laughed. Once he'd recovered he grinned at CeCe, "I promise not to blab to your *spooky* sister on one condition. Take a shower with us before Tobi comes bursting through the door and drags us out into the night in pursuit of God only knows what."

THE SHOWER IN the West's penthouse was pure decadence. It reminded her of one she'd seen in a magazine a few months ago. That shower had been a virtual tropical paradise and CeCe had practically drooled over the pages. Her Master had almost caught her, but she'd managed to simply dog-ear the page and slide the book into the stack when he'd come into the room. She knew him too well, if he'd seen her lusting after the little slice of heaven he would have moved heaven and earth to make it a reality. God she loved him, but the man didn't understand that she loved him for who he was, not what he could do for her. Maybe she could tackle the beach house's master suite as a do-it-yourself project? Her mind was swirling with all the possibilities as she stepped into the room-sized shower. There were multiple rain showerheads pouring down from the ceiling in addition to a dozen or more heads disguised as rocks jutting from various heights in the rock walls. Two stone benches on either end provided more than enough fuel for her imagination.

Cam's deep voice warmed her ear, "What is going through that brilliant mind of yours, my sweet slave? I can practically hear your mind whirling around. Do you like the shower?"

"Yes, Master, very much. And I—well, I was thinking how I could remodel the one in the beach house and maybe add tropical plants. I did some remodeling to my apartment when I was in college, so I think I might be able to manage it." CeCe could hear how breathless she sounded and hoped he would attribute her blush to the hot water raining down on her.

"Hmmm, I'm not sure that's how Master Carl or I envisioned our time there. But I admit, remodeling the master bath is a great idea. Perhaps I can even add a few extra features that you might enjoy, I do know how you love watersports." CeCe felt her sex flood as her arousal skyrocketed, the man's voice was like sex set to sound. *That "I'm going to fuck you until your bones melt" voice makes me want to drop to my knees and offer him everything. But hell, who needs to offer when he is more than willing to demand it all and then some?*

Chapter Eleven

For the first time in years Cam felt the thrill of excitement and anticipation. He rarely got to surprise anyone and least of all Cecelia, because she never asked for anything. He swore she was the least demanding woman in the world and it was far more frustrating than he could have ever imagined. *How do you lavish someone with gifts if they don't want anything? What the hell good is all this damned money if I can't spoil her rotten?*

Thinking back on the day he'd seen her reading in the den, he smiled to himself. He'd known she hadn't heard him approach. She was usually so focused on him as her Master that he rarely found opportunities to watch her when her focus was not on pleasing him. Even after Chloe was born, he could count on one hand the number of times he'd been able to stand in the shadows and watch her rock their child during the hours before the sun rose. She'd been completely engrossed in the magazine spread across her knees, her face had been full of wonder as she'd drawn her fingers over the color photos that filled the slick pages. From his place in the doorway he hadn't been able to see what had her so enraptured. But the moment she'd heard him she had quickly folded over the corner of the page to mark her place before sliding the book under several others and then dropping to her knees with her palms resting on her wide spread thighs.

Cam hadn't demanded she show him what she had attempted to hide, he'd simply waited until she'd left for work the next morning to look for himself. He'd recognized the incident for what it was, just one more symptom their relationship wasn't meeting all of her needs. When he'd seen the tropical paradise-inspired bathroom, he'd known exactly how to make that dream a reality. Now he could hardly wait for her to see the renovations he'd just completed at the beach house.

"I am looking forward to our vacation, pet. But I don't want to waste our time now thinking about what's to come, I want to enjoy *this* moment also." He turned her, pulling her back against his abdomen. He'd often forgot how tiny she was and she'd obviously lost quite a lot of weight in recent weeks, something else he'd be monitoring very closely while they were vacationing. He looked over to see the head of Carl's cock pointing straight up as if its purplish hue might persuade its owner to relieve some of the pressure. Looking up, Cam was surprised to see his friend's eyes focused on his own rather than the lush woman standing naked in front of him.

"Pet, I want you to bend at the waist and spread your legs for me. Push that sweet ass up so your pussy is open to your Master. And while I fuck you, you'll serve Master Carl."

"Yes, Master."

When she started to bend, he tightened the arm he had wrapped just under her breasts, "And I want you to give him one of your special massages, pet. Two fingers. Let's begin to prepare for what we all want, shall we?" Carl's eyes blazed with lust so strong Cam felt as if he might burst into flames. *Just wait until our little sub gets her fingers inside your ass, my friend. She is going to send you into space. Our lady might be a pediatric surgeon, but she knows exactly how and where to press those sweet fingers of her. You'll be lucky to remain on your feet, buddy.*

Cecelia nodded quickly and hurried into position as if she feared Carl might change his mind. Cam could have assured her he wouldn't, but he didn't bother. Now that Cam knew Carl hadn't ever submitted to another man, he could hardly wait to top his friend again. He didn't plan to top them both until they were safely inside their St. Maarten estate. Both he and Cecelia referred to it as a beach house, and *technically* that was true, even though it was probably misleading. But the entire property included two additional homes, one was occupied by the couple who cared for the house and grounds, the other was a combination guest/safe house.

The underground tunnel connecting the guesthouse to the main house had been one of the property's major selling points, it was also one of its best-kept secrets. The advance team Cam had sent to the island reported all the upgrades had been completed and there wasn't any place safer for a thousand miles in any direction. When he'd first purchased the property, the house had been lovely, but dated. He'd made improvements steadily over the years trying to maintain a balance between keeping the locals employed and happy versus alienating them by making too many changes too quickly.

Pushing himself into her slick sheath nearly caused his knees to buckle. Her body was hot and her pussy was soaked with sweet desire. Hearing Carl's groan as she took him to the back of her throat let Cam know he wasn't the only one who would be struggling to maintain their control. Cam leaned forward enough to gain another half inch and sighed when he felt the tip of his cock press against her womb's opening. "Jesus, you are so hot, pet. You undo me."

He watched as she nudged Carl's legs further apart and he saw his friend's eyes widen as she slid her small hand between his legs. "Holy fucking hell." Carl's startled words sounded as if they'd been growled rather than spoken. Having been on the receiving end of this particular "gift", Cam knew exactly what Carl was feeling.

"Let her pleasure you. She is going to rock your world. Brace your arms against the walls." Carl raised a brow and Cam laughed, "Trust me." In order to properly brace himself, Carl had to move his legs apart even more and Cecelia didn't miss the window of opportunity. Taking advantage of his distraction, she had obviously slid a second finger inside Carl's anus.

"*Fuck!* Jesus, Joseph, and Mary. Baby, you are playing with fire here. You are going to—" Carl's words cut off and Cam watched as Carl began to implode. The muscles lining Cecelia's pussy began rippling before he'd even started the pounding pace he knew would launch her over with both of them.

Carl was already shouting his release when Cam yelled, "Come—both of you come now." Cecelia nearly choked on the jets of Carl's release hitting the back of her throat when she tried to scream as her release swamped her at his command. Cam only outlasted them by a fraction of a second. His release had come on so quickly he had barely had time to order theirs before he'd been pulled under by the tidal wave that slammed into him. He slid his feet further apart to keep from tumbling forward and sending them all to the floor like falling dominos.

Somewhere beyond the roaring in his ears, Cam heard Carl softly praising Cecelia, "Baby, you almost burned me alive. I'm not sure I'm going to survive you." He pulled her up into his arms and held her against his chest while Cam tried to catch his own breath. *Christ al-fucking-mighty, the two of them are going to kill me.*

CeCe hadn't been able to move for several minutes, but the pounding on their bedroom door brought her out of the sex-drunk stupor she'd been languishing in. Carl's chest shook with his soft laughter, "That would be Tobi. Told you we didn't have long." He handed her back to Cam and stepped from the shower. Once he was dry, he held open a large towel and Cam set her outside the shower. *Thank God we'd finished, I don't even want to think about how loud we must have been.*

Once they'd dressed, she let Cam lead her out to the living room. All the men had sly smiles, but were polite enough not to mention them screaming the walls down a few minutes earlier. Tobi wasn't nearly as tactful. "Holy hot cakes, that must have been some nap. I'm sure that must have done wonders for your…um, well, stress level. Yeah, that's the ticket. I'm sure that was a great stress relief. Hells bells and cotton balls who needs sleep when you're getting bangin' sex, right?"

"Tobi." Kyle's growled warning fell on deaf ears.

"What? I didn't ever use any bad words. Hell is in the Bible, so it doesn't count." She'd crossed her arms under her ample breasts and stared at her husband. When he finally shook his head and turned away, Tobi looked at CeCe and winked. "I'm ready to go spend some money, what do you say? Your husband paid Gracie and I both a lot of money to set up those shops in his club and I can hardly wait to spend some of it."

As they made their way to the elevator, CeCe notice that she and Tobi were flanked on all sides by the men and wondered how they'd ever get any shopping done when she could barely see beyond the walls of hard male bodies they were enclosed in. Tobi must have noticed because she giggled, "Don't worry, they'll open up enough for us to see the clothes the owners have waiting for us. Lilly called ahead with our sizes and preferences, and if I know my friend and mother-in-law, we'll probably be treated like Queens." When CeCe laughed, Tobi looked over and grinned, "Oh, sister, you think I'm kidding and I am so *not*. You really haven't *shopped* until you have gone with Lilly. It's a whole new world. Heck, we even had beer and pizza delivered into one of So-Ho's chicest boutiques the last time we were here. It was awesome."

"Kitten, you might want to tell Cecelia how that ended." Kyle's words sounded pleasant enough, but CeCe heard the steel beneath them. Whatever had happened must have gotten Lilly and Tobi both in serious hot water.

Tobi's pretty face scrunched up and her hands unconsciously rubbed her backside. When CeCe looked up, every man in the elevator was fighting a smile. Their feeble attempts hadn't gone unnoticed by Tobi either. "Sure, you guys go ahead and laugh. But I will find out who the rat fink was…someday I'll find out and then I'm going to call up the hounds of hell, I promise you that." She looked over at Kyle and grinned, "Bible words are safe." CeCe giggled, earning her a glare and a wink from Kyle.

"Any *who,* there probably should have been more pizza and less beer, but well, in our defense it really was great beer. Whoever Lilly had called to deliver it brought some kick ass—ets stuff."

Tobi looked up at Kent, batting her eyes, he shook his head and chuckled, "I know the word ass is in the Bible, but I'm fairly certain that wasn't the way you intended. But, we'll leave that one open to negotiation. Now finish your story."

They had gotten off the elevator and made the short walk to the SUV and were almost out of the parking garage when CeCe saw Tobi's shoulders sag. "Okay, point taken. Well, one thing sort of led to another and we ended up dancing on the counter—in our underwear." CeCe gasped and her friend grinned. "Oh, it gets worse." She looked at Kent and then Kyle and shrugged, "Your dads really have incredible timing." Tobi returned her attention to CeCe and laughed, "Boy were they ever surprised when they walked in. They made sure to delete the videos on everybody's cameras and all the pictures, too. I don't even want to know how much they paid the management before we left, but the sales staff was sure anxious for us to come back again."

Kent chuckled, "I'm not sure I've ever seen the dads that mad. It was almost scary."

CeCe grinned at the pained look on Tobi's face, "You still don't know who tipped them off?"

"No. I could probably crack the code into NORAD before I'd get one of them to confess. But someday, somehow, someone will slip up, and then there won't be a hole deep enough for them to hide in. And I shudder to think what Lilly will do to them." By the time Tobi had finished her story, they'd stopped in front of a small boutique. As they were crawling out of the SUV, Tobi leaned over and whispered, "I'll dig the rat-bastard out and roast his nuts on a hickory stick over a campfire before I shoot him."

Tobi and CeCe both giggled until they heard Kyle's sharp voice behind them, "That's ten, kitten."

Kent leaned down and kissed her on the top of her blond head, "Aww, sweetness, you were so close, too." Everybody was still laughing as they entered the brightly lit store.

Chapter Twelve

Cameron watched as Cecelia and Tobi sorted through rack after rack of clothing. It was the first time in months he'd seen his lovely slave so relaxed and he was grateful Kent and Kyle had brought Tobi along. Looking to his side, Cam saw Kent grinning at the two women. "Thanks for bringing Tobi with you. I haven't seen Cecelia look this relaxed in far too long."

Kent turned and studied Cam so intently he was beginning to feel a bit like a bug under a microscope. Cam had known both West brothers for a long time because of their mutual friend, Jax McDonald, and the fact they'd all been members of the Special Forces at one time. But he still wasn't comfortable having the man watching him so closely, it was unnerving and he suddenly understood just how intimidating "the look" from a Dom could be. Cam finally raised a brow at his friend in silent question.

"What's really going on, Cam? You call us last week and casually mention you are thinking of moving and want to know if we'd be interested in buying Dark Desires. Then you call again two days ago needing help with a security threat involving your wife and child. And to be perfectly honest, that deal is fucked up seven ways to Sunday— nothing about that is adding up. Then when we set it up and Skype with you, letting you know who we're sending, every bit of color drains from your face when Carl's name is mentioned." *Fuck me, I know better than to react in front of men as observant as the Wests.*

Cam took a deep breath and then turned to Kent, "Carl and I knew one another years ago. We didn't part as enemies, but it wasn't pleasant either." Cam didn't want to spill the beans to Carl's boss, it wasn't his place. Nor did he want to put his own mistakes up on a stage, at least not until he knew exactly where this accidental trifecta was headed. Oddly enough, Kent didn't seem surprised. Kent simply nodded and Cam knew then the Wests' connections had once again prevailed. Shaking his head, Cam continued, "You don't seem surprised. And I honestly don't know why I thought you would be."

"Me either. You know our background checks go clear to the bone. We don't miss anything. Hell, we can't afford to miss anything. We're building a team that will be the absolute best at what they do. We'll be sending them into impossible situations and they need to know the people they are working with are golden. You know as well as I do that everything that happens to you or around you affects you in some way. Maybe it teaches you a lesson or maybe you have to experience it again and again for it to soak in, but each exposure makes a difference." Kent's words were spoken from a place of understanding, and Cam knew his friend was doing his best to avoid alienating him.

"Micah Drake?" Cam had heard about the security expert who was a part of the Prairie Winds' team. His computer hacking skills and military connections were practically legendary. When Kent shook his head, Cam felt his mouth drop open, "Jax?" He didn't even wait for Kent's answer, the answer was written all over his face. "How? How long?"

"I don't know, you'll have to ask him. But I want you

to stop and think about this, your friend has known this for years—hell, all of us have known for years, and no one has ever judged you or Carl. Jesus, we own fetish clubs that cater to a broad range of sexual preferences and kinks. We preach acceptance every damned day. Do you really think we are that hypocritical? That we'd tell our members to accept themselves and each other, but we'd judge you?" Kent's words were like a slap of self-awareness, because that was exactly what he'd been doing to himself. He'd watched men together in scenes a thousand times and never judged them, never considered treating them any differently, but he hadn't trusted anyone else would afford him the same consideration.

Cam was lost in his own thoughts as he rolled Kent's words over in his mind. Cecelia's easy acceptance when he'd confessed that he and Carl had enjoyed a physical relationship emphasized the enormity of his error. Kent sighed next to him and Cam couldn't help but cringe at the sound. Clearly the man thought he was dealing with someone with the I.Q. of a rock. "You know, Cam, the thing that really busts my ass in this whole thing is that you think so little of your friends. Might want to step out of that cold, stark fucking office now and then, buddy. Bet you'd be surprised how much you would enjoy the people around you." With that parting shot, Kent ambled toward his giggling wife.

WATCHING FROM THE shadows across the street from the clothing store where Cameron stood watching as his wife and Tobi West shopped, Craig breathed in the cool night air and smiled. *They thought I wouldn't know where they were*

going, but your friends aren't the only ones with computer skills, Cameron. He'd overheard his boss speaking to Fischer on the phone, thank God the club's manager hadn't actually been in the room. Craig avoided Fischer Weston at all costs, he was certain the man was possessed by the same demons Craig fought—the ones who could reach into a person's mind and steal his deepest thoughts. Not long after Craig had started working at the club, Fischer had walked by him and absently answered an unspoken question he'd been thinking over. The distracted manager hadn't even realized what he'd done, but a coworker had seen the exchange and joked that Master Weston could read minds. From that point forward, Craig made it a point to stay as far from the man as possible. He also made a concentrated effort to keep his mind on the task at hand anytime Weston was near.

Craig watched as Cameron talked to a man who he suspected was either Kyle or Kent West. Two of the men that entered the store with the group looked so much alike Craig doubted their own mother could tell them apart. Cameron had been practically drooling as he'd watched Cecelia look through clothing racks with Tobi West. Craig had met the bouncy blonde when she and Gracie McDonald helped the Dark Desires staff set up a few specialty shops several weeks ago. Both women had been friendly, but holy shit had they been able to trash an area in record time. They had teased him that he should demand a raise while they were there, and it was true because they had certainly made his job much more difficult. But they had also been so friendly and unassuming he'd found himself liking them despite their penchant for disorder.

Tobi had laughed at his need to keep the area spotless, telling him, "You are going to make yourself crazy trying to keep up, you know. We'll just pile up all the stuff and then you can get it at the end of the day."

He must have looked horrified, because her friend Gracie had burst out laughing. "It's okay, you know. If you want to keep us from breaking our necks tripping over all this, we'll be happy to let you handle it." Then she'd winked at him and added, "If she is going to turn this into tornado alley, she should at least spring for lunch. What shall we order, Mr. Allen?" Before he could answer, Gracie laughed, "But no alcohol. Tobi used to be a stripper and we'll have to turn off the radio if she drinks or she'll be dancing on the tables." Craig knew his chin had hit his chest, his mouth had dropped open so far.

"Gracie, you are a vile wench. I'm telling Jax and Micah that you are delusional and you'll be spending time with Dr. Freud if you aren't careful. And you know how Master Dan loves to poke around in the minds of submissives." Craig learned later that the man they'd been talking about was a well-respected and very successful psychologist in Austin. Dr. Dan Deal was also member of the Prairie Winds Club, but the two women didn't appear to really fear him. Too brave for their own good in his opinion. Damn, just the thought of dealing with another doctor made Craig shudder. He'd spent his entire life being shuttled between various doctors. Craig's parents had still been trying to "cure" him up to the night he'd watched them take their last breaths.

Just thinking about that night sent chills up his spine. It was the first time the demons in his head managed to drown out everything but their demands. He hadn't wanted to kill his mother and father, but they wouldn't listen to reason. Each time he'd tried to explain how much Cameron meant to him, they'd insisted he wasn't really "that way" and if he'd just see one more doctor...stay in one more facility for a few months, then he'd be "cured" and become the son they'd always dreamed he could be. Shaking off that memory, Craig refocused his attention on the group he'd been watching as the men loaded multiple packages into the back of the large SUV.

Craig slid down in the seat of his rental car when Cameron and Carl Phillips escorted Dr. Barnes out of the store. He didn't really want to have to hurt her, she'd always been nice enough to him. But she was an obstacle that had to be removed one way or another. Snapping pictures as the group moved to the vehicle's open doors, he focused on Cameron because something was different about the man he'd adored for nearly three decades. Craig knew he would spend hours analyzing the photos once he'd returned to his hotel room across from the tower where they were staying. He was able to follow at a safe distance because he'd been able to place a small tracking unit on the vehicle. It hadn't been easy, but there had been a few precious seconds when both of the men assigned to patrol outside had been at the opposite ends of the block. *Damn, they were pissed when I pretended to stagger into the side of their boss's precious ride. And fast, too. He'd barely had enough time to put the device in place before they'd reached his side.*

THEY HAD NO more than pulled away from the car when Kyle's phone rang. Carl wasn't sure who his boss was listening to, but it was easy to see Kyle was about a hot second from exploding. "Can you back trace it? Find out where it's going and let me know. Also tap into the exterior videos and those of the surrounding buildings to see if you can get his face." When he'd disconnected the call, Carl listened as Kyle recounted his conversation with Micah. No one doubted the tracking unit had been added by the man who'd bumped into the side of the SUV, but it had been dark enough and he had obviously been convincing enough the team members who had dealt with him hadn't thought to check his identification. Carl doubted it would have made any difference, the man wouldn't have been carrying his real ID anyway.

Carl knew the two Prairie Winds team members who had seen the man fall against the car regretted not confronting him, but in their defense, they'd been the only two on the street securing the entire perimeter. From what Carl had heard, it was doubtful they could have gotten to him before he'd made the stick anyway. Kyle watched as Tobi unfastened her seatbelt and leaned forward to speak to Ben Monroe. Carl hadn't met Ben before coming to Prairie Winds but had heard the six-foot block of muscle had been a college power lifter prior to joining the military. The man had opted out after witnessing a bloody massacre of women and children in Columbia. Kent had told him Ben still struggled with bouts of PTSD but those incidents were far less frequent now. Tobi West had a heart the size of her home state and she'd obviously known Ben would shoulder the blame and feel as though he'd put both she and CeCe in danger. He couldn't hear what she said to Ben, but it had obviously helped because he could see the other man's shoulders relax as he took a deep breath and nodded.

When Tobi slid back into her seat, Kyle ran his fingers down the side of her face and whispered something to her that brought tears to her eyes before kissing her so thoroughly Cam finally told them to get a room. With the tension broken, the girls started plotting their strategy for their next stop while Kent and Kyle turned to Carl and Cameron. "Micah is already commandeering the cams surrounding our next stop. It's not the greatest location for video and I'd change our plans if we hadn't gotten these places to open up in the middle of the damned night for us."

Kent shook his head, "Whoever is following us might already know where we were going anyway. If we changed things up, we'd risk spooking him. The tracker may be for later since these two stops really are the only things we had planned while everybody was in town." Carl agreed with Kent, they couldn't vary their routine much from the last stop or they'd send up red flags quickly.

This time Cam stayed inside with CeCe while Carl wandered around outside looking as if he was just shooting the breeze with Mitch and Ben. They'd used the large coffee shop across the street as an excuse to look around and noted a couple of cars that had someone seated in the driver's seat, but only one caught their interest. As soon as they approached, the man inside jumped out of the car and took off down the street. Tossing aside the tray he was carrying, Mitch took off in pursuit as Carl sprinted back to the boutique.

CAM HEARD CARL'S shout to secure the area as he ran through the front door. He didn't bother to ask why, he just ushered CeCe, Tobi, and the sales staff in the dressing rooms and closed the door with promises of punishment if they left the area. The wide-eyed response he'd gotten from the young sales staff almost made him laugh. Before he'd stepped away from the door he'd heard one ask if he was serious. "Oh yeah, he's very serious. Trust me, you don't want to test him on this." He smiled at his sweet slave's words to the others, they would do well to heed her warning.

Carl met him at the front of the building and Cam didn't miss the fact his friend positioned himself between Cam and the windows. "It's too easy. I'm worried he was a decoy meant to lure us out of the store. Are you carrying?"

Cam nodded, "Always."

"Good to know. I'll cover the front, it's too exposed for you."

Before Carl could say any more, Mitch walked in shaking his head. "Fuck! The kid I chased four damned blocks was paid to sit in the car and take off if anyone approached. He said the guy who hired him was—and I quote, 'not a big guy, with sorta brown hair maybe, and not really tall'. Yeah, there's a description not worth jack shit."

Ben was standing behind him grinning, "Well, it didn't help that you scared him so bad he pissed his pants, either. Fuck man, you scared me and I'm usually the one terrifying women and children."

Kyle shook his head at the men before turning, speaking to the small group gathered around him, "As soon as we get the all clear from Micah we're out of here. We'll scramble the tracker's signal, but I'm betting whoever was on the other end already knows where we're staying. We will not be leaving that facility until we escort the Barnes to the airport."

"I assume we'll be scrubbing those plans as well?" Cam knew the routine well, but wanted to make sure he and Kyle were on the same page.

"Absolutely. Jax is working on that from Prairie Winds, but I know he's working with his dad also. Who knows whose jet he'll hijack for you, hell, between our dads and his, it's a crap shoot, but I'll bet it's a nice ride." Everyone around knew Kyle's words were a classic understatement, because the elder Wests and McDonalds were well known for enjoying their creature comforts. Cam smiled and nodded.

By the time they'd stepped back to the safety of the penthouse, Cecelia was pasty white and shaking like a leaf. Carl had been detained downstairs dealing with the electronic tracker, Kyle wanted to meet with all of the men in his office, and Cam wanted to growl with frustration. Knowing he was going to have to leave Cecelia alone for a few minutes didn't set well with him at all. She'd been working unholy hours for months and Cam knew she had been looking forward to this vacation for weeks, and now some ass hat was destroying it. He didn't feel like he was doing a very good job of taking care of his sweet slave and that admission made him realize just how valuable a ménage arrangement might be.

Cam stopped at the door to tell Kent he would join them as soon as he settled Cecelia in their room and just as he stepped into the large living room, he saw her stumble, and before he could take the extra few steps to reach her, she was falling. Time slowed and he felt as if he was watching the entire scene unfold from a distance. It had taken just a split second for him to see what was coming and there was no way he could possibly make it to her in time. As long as he lived, Cam was sure he'd never forget the sound of her head hitting the steel edged end table.

Chapter Thirteen

CeCe felt like she was swimming through Jell-O. A small part of her brain knew she'd been hurt, she'd talked to too many patients who had described this exact feeling to her, it was impossible to not recognize it. But the biggest part of her mind was screaming *what the fuck happened?* God it hurt to think, she wanted to slide back into sleep but someone was talking to her. Whoever it was kept insisting that she should wake up and let them look at her pupils. *Seriously? I'm a doctor, I know you are going to shine a friggin' spotlight in my eyes and it's going to feel like someone has skewered my brain with a red-hot poker...so thanks, but no thanks. Believe I'll pass on the hot sword behind the eyes treatment but it was nice of you to offer. Now leave me the hell alone. Maybe I'll feel better when I wake up sometime next week.*

"Come on, pet, you need to wake up and talk to the doctor. He promises to scale back the spotlight. And the sooner you cooperate the sooner we can leave for the beach house. What do you say?" Cam? Was it really him? His voice was so soft and soothing, not at all harsh or demanding. He'd sounded so worried her submissive nature would not allow her to put her comfort above his. CeCe tried to open her eyes and felt her forehead crinkle from the effort, but her eyelids felt as if they were taped down. She felt his fingers threaded through hers and she tightened her fingers hoping he'd know she was listening.

The effort to open her eyes was excruciating and she felt herself sliding back into the abyss. Just as she slipped into the blissful oblivion of unconsciousness, she heard the doctor say, "Let her rest. We know she could hear you and that tells us a lot." She would have smiled at his words if it hadn't required so much effort. *Please don't worry, Master.*

She didn't know how long she'd been asleep, but this time CeCe's eye's fluttered open on their own. It took a couple of minutes for everything to come into focus and her head still throbbed with what had to be a headache sent straight from the depths of hell. Before the room came fully into focus, she felt warm fingers lace into her cold ones. "Welcome back, sweetness." Carl's softly spoken words warmed her heart and she felt tears fill her eyes. She didn't know why she suddenly felt so emotional, and he must have sensed her unease. "It's okay, baby, the doctor said your emotions might swing wildly for a while, so don't feel bad when that happens, okay?"

"Yes, Sir." Her head was ready to explode, but she wasn't going to risk answering a Dom disrespectfully. No need to add a stinging ass to her throbbing head.

Carl lowered the side rail on the bed and sat next to her. The warm fingers of one hand tangled with hers as he used his other hand to brush her hair to the side. "Cam just left a couple of minutes ago to get some coffee. I'm guessing his absence is what woke you, and I have to say I envy him that soul deep connection." She wondered if what he'd said was true. Could she be so connected to her Master that she'd awakened when he'd left the room? Carl's fingers brushed softly over her wrinkled brow, "Don't look so worried. A trust that deep is a beautiful gift, and it's one I know he treasures above all else." She felt herself relax as she listened to his explanation. Viewing it as having felt safe in his presence was so much better than feeling dependent. She watched as something resembling envy flashed in his eyes before he masked it. "Knowing the woman who held my heart felt that safe in my presence would be the sweetest gift she could give me." Looking into the depths of his Caribbean blue eyes, CeCe realized how much she wished she could be that woman even though her desire didn't make any sense. *Good Lord, Cecelia, get a flippin' grip. Don't be putting the cart before the horse.* She could almost hear her sweet granny's words echoing through her mind.

He was probably just trying to soothe her until he could get back to watching out for her. It seemed ironic that she needed a bodyguard but she'd actually done the most damage to herself. "Now, tell me where you hurt. I can see the pain etched in your face, let's see if we can't ease that a bit before your Master storms back in here thinking I've put that frown on your pretty face."

His shift in direction surprised her and she blinked at him a couple of times trying to focus on what he'd said. *Why can't I seem to follow even the simplest conversation?* "I'm sorry, I don't seem to be fully cognizant just yet. I'm really not usually this dull, I swear."

His soft chuckle put her at ease, "Sweetness, you have a very nasty concussion. I'd be more surprised if you weren't struggling a bit to keep up. Now, what's hurting you so much it's draining the energy right out of you?"

"My head. It feels like it's going to explode." She hated how thin her voice sounded. She'd never been one to give in to weakness easily, but damn her head hurt so bad she was worried she might throw up.

Carl picked up a glass of water she hadn't noticed and positioned the straw to her lips, "Take several small sips.

Let's start by rehydrating you. I'm sure as a physician you well know the connection between hydration and headaches, but it's awfully easy to forget the basics when you are the patient." CeCe did know, but just as he'd said, she hadn't even thought to take a couple drinks of water. When she'd finished he set the glass aside and began massaging her right hand. "You are right handed, correct?" When she nodded he smiled and continued, paying particular attention to the space between her thumb and forefinger. She flinched when he hit a particularly tender spot and he looked up into her eyes, "That's the spot, now lean back and breathe through this for me." Before she'd even gotten into position, he pressed firmly on the tender spot he'd identified and held it tightly between his fingers for so long she was almost panting to keep from pulling back. But when he released her hand she was shocked to find her headache wasn't nearly as severe as it had been just a few minutes earlier.

Like most physicians, she didn't feel like she knew nearly enough about alternative medical treatments. Medical schools didn't emphasize those and once doctors reached residency, they were so overwhelmed and exhausted there wasn't time to add anything else to their plates. Perhaps someday she would be able to scale back her schedule enough to allow her time to study some of the more popular methods because clearly there were things her patients could benefit from. Carl slipped his hands on either side of her neck so the pads of his middle fingers pressed solidly against the spots at the base of her skull she knew were referred to as the "Gates of Consciousness." Her headache had already abated enough that this time she felt an immediate flood of relief and for the first time since she'd opened her eyes she wasn't worried the nausea was going to overwhelm her.

She hadn't realized her eyes had closed until she heard Cam's voice, "Is she alright?"

"Yes, she had a bad headache and I know they won't give her anything for it because of the concussion, so I was using acupressure to help alleviate some of the pain." He'd been gently massaging her neck and the tender place where her spine disappeared into her skull—*just a few more seconds and I'll be able to slide back into the oblivion of sleep.* "But if I don't stop now she's going to go back to sleep and I'd rather the doctor visited with her and we're able to get her out of here. This place is a nightmare to defend, we'll be far safer at the penthouse." *Fuck me. So close, too.*

CARL HAD WATCHED CeCe start to stir as soon as the door closed behind Cam. He wondered if the man he'd once considered his best friend had any idea what an incredible gift he'd been given when Cecelia agreed to belong to him. She'd instinctively felt safe enough to sleep while he was in the room, but the moment he'd stepped out, she'd become restless. Carl dimmed the lights and moved to the side of her bed knowing it wasn't going to be long until she awoke in the strange room and he didn't want her to be frightened. She'd surprised him by fighting through the pain he knew she had to be experiencing. He'd had his share of concussions and knew the headache that followed could be debilitating.

He'd seen soldiers who continued to fight during firefights despite being shot several times, men who were later flattened by the bloody headache that followed a closed head injury. It didn't surprise him the NFL and other sports organizations were finally being forced to recognize the seriousness of the injuries they'd so often blatantly disregarded. It was obvious CeCe was accustomed to working through discomfort. He watched as she tried to bring her surroundings into focus and he stood perfectly still knowing any movement on his part would likely have her doubled over heaving her heels. When he threaded his fingers through hers, he was surprised to feel her trembling and not in the way a Dom enjoyed. Her face was so pale it was almost translucent and within seconds he saw beads of perspiration form on her forehead. The skin on her tiny hand felt clammy in his much larger one, he knew she was close to losing it.

As Carl watched CeCe struggle with the headache she'd said felt like it was going to make her head explode, he remembered watching a teammate ease a fellow soldier's pain with touch alone. The kid had been thrown against a concrete wall by the explosive force of a car bomb detonated in the street as their group had been exiting a building. While their team was pinned down the young man's incoherent ramblings had threatened to give away their position, but he'd been so blinded by the pain no one had been able to reason with him.

Carl remembered watching Taz work while explaining patiently that he'd learned the technique from his Sioux grandmother. He'd explained a lot more about the energy pathways of the body and how interrupting those carrying pain messages could ease a patient's suffering, but Carl couldn't remember all the details. But the little bit he had been able to recall had helped CeCe, and that's all that mattered. He was grateful his Native American friend and teammate had been willing to share the information, seeing the relief in her pretty dark eyes had gone a long way to begin convincing her she was safe in his care.

Thinking about Taz made Carl smile. His name was actually Tashunka Ledek, and it hadn't taken his fellow SEALs long to find out his first name was a traditional Sioux name meaning horse. The team had teased him relentlessly that it was far too easy to see *why* his parents had chosen that particular moniker because the man was enormous—all over. At six foot five Taz was intimidating, but when you added his dark coloring and SCARS skills, he was downright terrifying. Taz had earned his nickname as a deadly street fighter in and around various military bases around the world. When his dad got tired of pulling his son's ass out of the fire, he enrolled the young man in various martial arts classes.

From the stories that circulated through the teams, Carl knew Taz had practically sailed through the SEALs Special Combat Aggressive Reactionary Systems mixed martial arts training because it utilized skills from all the methods he'd already been using for years. The last time he and Taz had worked together, Taz had mentioned he was studying Krav Maga. The fighting method had been developed for the security services of Israel, its use of leverage made it deadly and effective no matter the fighter's height. Adding those particular skills to an already fully loaded arsenal of abilities was going to make Taz almost unstoppable in hand-to-hand situations. Carl made a mental note to ask the Wests if they had considered bringing Taz on board their rapidly expanding team.

He'd heard Cam enter the room and had been grateful CeCe's Master had waited quietly to the side while he'd worked. When he looked up into Cam's eyes Carl had been surprised to see not only gratitude but a simmering lust as well. Later, as they stood in the hallway while the elderly doctor examined CeCe, Cam asked, "Where did you learn to do that?"

Kent West was standing on Cam's other side and grinned, "I'd be willing to bet a bundle on Taz Ledek. Honestly, I've never met anyone else having as wide and as varied range of skills as he does. I remember our CO swearing Taz learned a whole new set of professional skills annually just to keep from having to sit still." Carl laughed to himself because he'd heard the commanding officer make that observation on several occasions, and the bottom line was—it was probably more accurate than any of them knew.

The doctor reluctantly released CeCe into their care, but made it clear he was only doing so because they'd all had medic training during BUD/S. The six-month Basic Underwater Demolition/SEAL training was among the toughest in the world and the doctor's concession was a nod to that famously rigorous regime. It hadn't taken the men long to return CeCe to the penthouse once she'd been discharged—hell, it had taken longer to get Tobi out of their room after settling their injured woman in bed. Tobi had been in full *mommy-mode* and fussed over her friend until Kent had simply wrapped his arm around her waist, picked up the petite blonde, and walked from the room. Carl saw CeCe grin just before her eyes slid closed.

Chapter Fourteen

CECE LOOKED OUT the tinted window of the black SUV wondering how the men had managed to arrange what she'd considered a small military operation rather than a trip to the airport in just under twenty-four hours. Where had all these people come from anyway? These were the moments she appreciated how little she really understood about Cameron's background. Seeing him in *operative-mode* was so different from the Master that she knew and loved. As an operative he was authoritative, but a team player to the bone. She wasn't accustomed to seeing him compromise and defer to others, and the transformation in his appearance and personality were amazing to watch.

God in heaven, it had been hard to say goodbye to Tobi this morning. They'd promised to do a better job of keeping in touch and Tobi's men had promised to bring her for a visit as soon as it was safe to do so. CeCe hadn't realized how much she had missed having a friend close at hand, but the past few days had reminded her of the importance of that connection. *I really have to start living my life before I wake up and realize it's passed by and all I have to show for it is a career that drove me into a state of utter exhaustion.*

One of her biggest fears had always been that her baby was going to grow up with Cam and various nannies, but without the influence of the woman who had given birth to her. Just thinking about her baby girl made her heart clench. She'd seen her more on her small tablet screen in the past few days than she had in person for several months, and even though she hadn't been able to "touch" her, she'd still read her stories and listened to her babble in response. Watching her daughter sleeping in her sister's arms had warmed Chloe's heart even as it was breaking from all she was missing.

CeCe felt her safety belt release just as she was pulled into a warm embrace. She hadn't even realized she'd been crying until Carl turned her face to his and brushed her tears away with the pads of his fingers. "Talk to me." On a cognitive level, CeCe knew patients suffering closed head trauma were often unpredictably emotional after their injury, but this felt different—even if it wasn't. She didn't know how she was going to explain what had brought on her feelings of melancholy.

Cam was sitting in the front passenger's seat, when he turned and smiled at her, CeCe was relieved he wasn't angry with her. She'd talked to Tobi and Gracie both for hours about how the men in their lives handled the whole "sharing" thing but she'd never truly believed it could work until she'd seen the West brothers with Tobi these past few days. Even then, she'd assumed their relationship was unique because Kyle and Kent were twins. In her mind, they'd been sharing things since the womb, so it was reasonable to expect them to deal with the obvious challenges with much more ease. But now, seeing Cam's easy acceptance of Carl's affection for her, CeCe wondered if it might not be possible to have a similar relationship. *What the hell are you thinking? You were just crying because you don't make time to spend with your baby, and now you're thinking about taking on two men?* Cripes, if she kept this up, men in white jackets were going to meet them at the airport, strap her into a straightjacket, and haul her off to the cracker factory.

Carl's soft voice sounded close to her ear and the warmth of his breath against its shell sent a wave of heat through her, "Baby? Why the tears? I know concussions can knock even the strongest people off their feet emotionally, but I've got a feeling this is more than that." He pulled her face to his and kissed the tip of her nose so sweetly she felt a new rush of tears streaming down her cheeks.

"I'm sorry, Sir. I was just having a *moment*. I'll be fine." She wasn't used to such a show of compassion from a Dom. Even though she loved her Master, he'd never been the type to hold her in his arms just because she'd had a bad day. He was much more likely to take her into his personal playroom at the club or at home, and make her forget everything but how quickly he could send her into sub-space. Just the evening before they'd left, Cam had entered the bedroom and seen her staring out the large window. She'd been worrying her lower lip and he'd known immediately she was beginning to drown in worry.

Her Master had promptly moved her into position, bent her over the large bed, pulled up her dress and paddled her ass until she hadn't been able to hold back the tears any longer. Once she'd vented the frustration, he'd fucked her with long pounding strokes meant to remind her that she was his to care for and the orgasm he'd given her had buckled her knees. She wasn't sure Cam knew another way to deal with her when she was emotional, but some part of her soul recognized Carl would be much different. In that split second after she'd spoken the lie, she regretted not taking a chance with him.

As if sensing her internal struggle, Carl shifted her on his lap and then grinned at her hiss of discomfort. "Baby, I told you I was as dominant as Cam—we just handle things differently...most of the time. I'm going to give you one chance to amend that lie you just told me."

For the first time CeCe sensed the inner strength of the man holding her. Oh, he might appear to be carefree, but there was an iron will at his core, that much she knew for certain. Riding in a vehicle with three Doms, following at least two other SUVs with Doms inside, all the while being followed by who knew how many vehicles with Doms in them seemed like a very inopportune moment to test the resolve of the Dom holding her on his lap. She squirmed and froze when she felt his very erect, very large cock pressing against her ass. CeCe hadn't even realized she wasn't even breathing until she heard Carl's voice against her ear, "Better take a breath, baby, before you pass out. And yes, I want you—but I do have enough control over my cock to get through this conversation." His voice was so calm and laced with such sincerity, CeCe felt herself relax into him. "Now, tell me the truth about what caused those tears."

CeCe took a deep breath as she laid her head against his shoulder. God the man was hard everywhere, his arms felt like bands of steel wrapped around her as she sat on his muscular thighs. And she wasn't even going to *go there* about the enormous iron rod pressing into her hip. "I was thinking about how I've gotten myself so caught up in building my practice and clinic that I've forgotten why I wanted to be a physician. My Master and daughter are paying for that selfishness in ways I'm just beginning to understand." She felt a new flood of tears, but she forced herself to take a steadying breath and continue, "The part that scares me is that I'm not even sure how to fix it at this point. The clinic itself has become like some living, breathing, energy-sapping Goliath. Last week I was so buried under administrative paperwork that I was only able to operate twice, and both of those were procedures for patients I hadn't even met personally."

This time she didn't even try to stem the flow of tears, "That is just awful. I never wanted to be one of those doctors who didn't know their patients. In the beginning I knew them all by name. I knew their parents' names, their siblings, and the grandparents. I knew what their goals were, and I helped them get there."

Cam turned in his seat and handed Carl a soft cotton handkerchief, her Master always teased her that he carried them because the gender that needed them the most never seemed to have one handy. When she quietly murmured her thanks, he simply nodded at her but she didn't miss the look that passed between the two men and she had the strangest feeling they were secretly pleased with her revelation. CeCe mopped up her "leaky" self and laid her head back on Carl's shoulder, she was exhausted—both physically and emotionally. Promising herself that she would just sleep until they reached the plane was the last thought she had before sliding into blissful slumber.

CARL FELT THE sweet woman in his arms lay her head against his shoulder and nuzzle her face against the side of his neck just before she went limp in his arms. His heart squeezed with the realization that she felt safe in his embrace. Holding her was sweet torture but he had no intention of putting her back in her own seat. He'd known she was petite, but hadn't really understood how small she was until she'd cuddled against him like an injured kitten seeking the warmth she needed to heal. Even though her words had been spoken quietly against his ear, he knew Cam had heard them all. CeCe evidently hadn't considered the earbud communication device he was wearing would transmit her confession to the entire team.

Their security detail might be made up of former operatives, but they were still fathers, husbands, brothers, and sons who cared deeply for the women in their lives, so he was sure her pained words had affected each of them. Carl had noticed a long time ago that the most hardened soldiers on the outside were often the most compassionate when you managed to move past their crusty exteriors.

The drive to the airport passed quickly and he'd enjoyed holding the precious armful of woman far more than he probably should have. Carl needed to remember that protecting her had to come first. It wasn't that he was opposed to exploring a ménage relationship—but until they found out who was threatening her, he needed to keep his priorities straight. *Keep telling yourself that, Phillips. And I'm sure you can find a nice seaside resort in western Texas, too.*

Carl settled the sleeping angel he'd carried on to the King Air they'd be taking to St. Maarten in one of the soft leather seats. He had to give Jax credit, the jet would probably put most four-star hotels to shame. The only thing missing was the pool and hot tub, and he wouldn't be surprised to find the later in the back. After reclining her seat and buckling her in, Carl covered her with a cashmere throw Cam handed him. "She'd incredible, isn't she?" Cam's voice was almost reverent as he looked down on CeCe.

"She is indeed. You're a very lucky man." Carl turned to walk away, but Cam grabbed his arm turning him back to face him. His friend's brow raised in question, he'd obviously heard the unspoken words in Carl's tone. "Her safety needs to be my first concern, once she's safe, I'll be able to consider your offer." With that, Carl turned and found his bag before settling in a seat on the other side of the luxurious jet. Opening his laptop, he tried to get some work done but his gaze kept straying to the beautiful woman sleeping so peacefully across the cabin from him.

Long, dark lashes lay serenely atop the dark circles under her eyes. The contrast between angelic beauty and heartbreaking sadness made Carl's heart clench with the need to protect her. He might be on assignment to guard her against a threat from the outside, but his gut told him the biggest threat to her safety and happiness was from herself.

Once again reviewing the before and after pictures he'd been sent of the beach house, Carl was impressed with the changes Cam had made to the small bungalow. Well, it wasn't exactly small anymore, the recent remodeling had nearly doubled the square footage, but surprisingly from the outside it didn't look that much different. Additional underground safe rooms, offices, and a much larger dungeon had been carved out of the bedrock and provided a level of safety few would imagine without closer inspection. But Carl's favorite change was the long veranda stretching the length of the enormous master suite on the newly added top level. The view over the ocean was spectacular even in photos and Carl could hardly wait to see it in person.

"The remodeling you've done is going to make your beach home much easier to defend. It's well planned and from what I can tell, the work looks like it's been done right." Carl wasn't lying, it appeared Cam had used skilled craftsmen and he had to wonder what it had cost to ship in those people.

"The most remarkable part of this project is all of that work was done using local labor. The talent on that small island is mind boggling." Cam's eyes had been focused on CeCe as he spoke and when they shifted to Carl there was a vulnerability there that Carl couldn't remember ever seeing before. "It's my hope that once this situation is resolved you'll consider staying." Carl felt his eyebrows raise in surprise and Cam chuckled softly from his seat across the wide aisle. "We'll talk more about it after we get to the house. I have a brilliant plan." His voice had dropped and the look of vulnerability was replaced by the devilish grin Carl remembered was always a signal his friend had likely cooked up a scheme that would leave the earth scorched around them. Years ago those plans had gotten them in more trouble than Carl wanted to think about.

Instead of pressing for information, Carl simply nodded and returned to his work. It would be a long trip and he'd have plenty of time to rest later—after he managed to tame the raging hard-on threatening to topple the small computer off his lap.

Chapter Fifteen

CAM LIFTED HIS sleeping slave into his arms and with a quick jerk of his head letting Carl know he wanted him to follow, Cam made his way to the jet's bedroom. They still had plenty of time to enjoy the perks of flying in luxury and Cam saw no reason to waste the opportunity. He'd been watching Cecelia sleep for several hours and when she began shifting restless in the reclined seat he knew it was time to wake her up with a smile.

"Come on, my sleepy pet, your Masters want to play with you a bit. Let's get you undressed first, shall we?" He set her on her feet but kept a tight hold on her as Carl lifted her short dress over her head. *Yes indeed, this is reason enough to forbid undergarments forever.* He'd always hated panties and had paddled Cecelia's ass for wearing them so many times when he'd first collared her, Cam had started to wonder if she was disobeying him deliberately. One night after a particularly harsh spanking, he'd asked her why she simply refused to stop wearing the offending garments. She'd tearfully explained that she often had to dress and undress in front of other medical staff in the locker room before and after surgery, and she just couldn't face doing that without underwear. From then on he'd made accommodations for that circumstance, but he'd given her several additional swats for not explaining her dilemma earlier.

Cam wasn't sure he would ever feel love the same way other people seemed to, he'd certainly never seen it modeled at home while growing up. Everything in the Barnes mansion was about the public's perception. His parents had firmly believed it didn't matter if they were actually *doing* the right thing, it was only important that it appeared as though they were. In their opinion, as long as they were listed at the top of the donor list for all the right local charities and were photographed at A-list parties, everything was copasetic. Their life behind closed doors was chaotic to say the least.

Cameron made the unfortunate decision to come home early for Christmas break and walked in on a drug-fueled orgy that would have made the ancient Roman Emperor Nero proud. He'd stood in the doorway watching his father fucking his best friend's wife while his mother was being pummeled by a device he later learned was called a "plow" as several men and women watched. The things he'd seen that night as a sixteen year old had made their judgment two years later all the more hypocritical.

Everyone in attendance had been so high he'd gone completely unnoticed, as far as Cam knew, Thomas, his parent's butler, was still the only person who knew he'd been there that night. The stoic Brit had worked for Cam's grandparents before being reassigned to Cam's parents. A few years ago Cam had contacted the man who had been the closest thing to a father he'd ever known. Cam had encouraged Thomas to retire and helped him move to St. Maarten to live in the small guest cottage behind the beach house. Smiling to himself, Cam knew Cecelia was looking forward to seeing the elderly man again, they'd hit it off immediately as he'd known they would. Thomas no longer worked but enjoyed island life, and from what Cam had heard, the ninety-two year old was still active and as sharp-witted as ever.

Carl had stripped quickly and started the water while Cam walked Cecelia into the large shower. The doctor who had treated Cecelia had warned them she would probably be unsteady for several days so he and Carl made sure one of them kept their hands on her at all times. Cam handed her off to Carl and watched as his friend's eyes softened as he enfolded her in his embrace. It was easy to see the man was already falling for the lovely woman, and that wouldn't be surprising for anyone who knew Cecelia. She was the most genuine person Cam had ever met. Her heart was open and honest, he couldn't recall a moment when he'd ever seen her be insincere. His only worry was that Carl might not be able to handle the relationship Cam envisioned for the three of them. But as his friend had said earlier, ensuring her safely had to come first. There would be time to discuss everything else later—right now it was all about keeping Cecelia and Chloe safe.

He took his time getting out of his clothes, watching as Carl rubbed circles over Cecelia's back while murmuring softly against her ear was pure eroticism. Cam had always considered himself something of a voyeur, it was one of his needs that had been filled by owning the club. But in all the years he'd spent watching the pleasure of others, he'd never seen anything that turned him on as much as the scene playing out in front of him now. He wasn't sure if they were swaying to something Carl was singing against her ear or if the movement was due to the jet's gentle shifts, but it was completely mesmerizing.

Cecelia's entire body seemed softer, more relaxed under Carl's touch. This contrast was exactly what Cam had felt she'd needed, and watching the two of them together confirmed his suspicion. When he'd first considered a permanent ménage relationship a couple of years earlier, the surge of possessiveness he'd felt had surprised him so he'd set the idea aside. But after spending time with his friends, he come to understand how much the arrangement benefitted all the parties involved. Jax McDonald and his best friend, Micah Drake, each brought different things into their relationship with Gracie. The same was true of Kent and Kyle West's relationship with their shared wife, Tobi.

The Wests' relationship was actually a better model for the trifecta he hoped to form with Cecelia and Carl. Kyle was harsher than his twin, his view of the world was generally very black and white, just as Cam's was. But Kent seemed to have been able to successfully blur the fine line between sexual Dominant and lover far better than Cam ever hoped to. And despite the fact everyone had noticed Kyle West had mellowed far more than any of them had ever expected, he was still much stricter than his brother. Cecelia was a lot like Tobi in that she needed both facets of the lifestyle in order to be happy.

He and Kyle had sat up late the night before last talking about how his and Kent's differing styles as Doms helped them meet Tobi's needs. Kyle had smiled as he looked out the bank of floor to ceiling windows making up one whole wall of the penthouse's huge living room. Kyle rolled the edge of his glass in slow circles on the arm of the leather chair, looking lost in thought for so long Cam wondered if he was going to respond. "You know, there are times when Tobi craves the discipline I provide, she thrives in a structured environment—strange as that may seem. But functioning on that level all the time is exhausting, both physically and emotionally, and it's when she finds herself in that emotional abyss that she turns to Kent. My brother is every bit the Dom I am, sometimes he is actually stricter, but he is far better at coaxing Tobi into compliance than I am. He knows how to hold her and just let her absorb his strength. I can't tell you how often I've walked up onto the terrace to find them just cuddled together on one of the loungers. Kent will be wearing nothing but soft flannel pants and he'll have our naked nymph against his bare chest. He swears skin-to-skin contact releases some kind of feel good chemical in the brain, so he just covers them both in a soft blanket."

"I'd have never taken Kent as a new-age enthusiast."

"You'd be surprised. My brother reads anything he can get his hands on, always has. But since we became husbands and fathers, his reading seems to center on anything he deems might make us better in those roles." Cam didn't hold back his chuckle because it was obvious the man was enjoying the perks of his brother's research, even if he didn't want to admit it. At one time Carl had been very much like Kent West and Cam wondered how much the years had changed his friend. Walking away from Carl Phillips that night had been one of the hardest things Cam had ever done, but he'd hoped to save his friend from the fall-out that was sure to follow if he didn't. As it turned out, Carl had too much integrity to live the lie Cam had given the school officials. By the time Cameron had found out what Carl had done it was too late, but refusing to contact Carl later was all on his shoulders.

Cam knew he came off as a hard ass. Hell, recently he'd been a jerk of epic proportions. Just last week his administrative assistant had reminded him that all the things he lectured others about were among his most annoying traits. He'd growled at her like a rapid dog, but in the end he'd known she was right. He felt himself slipping further and further away from the person he should be and he didn't like it one bit.

Sighing inwardly, he tried to shake off the direction his thoughts had gone and refocused his attention on Carl's hands as they stroked the globes of Cecelia's sweet ass. The contrast between his tanned fingers and her pale flesh made Cam wonder what those fingers would feel like as they wrapped around his own throbbing erection. He could hardly wait to feel Carl's tongue dipping into the slit for the pearly pre-cum that he could already feel beading at the tip of his cock. Pushing his shirt off his shoulders and shoving off his slacks, Cam stepped to the edge of the shower but stood back…watching.

CARL HAD SEEN Cam standing outside the shower and wondered if he intended to join them or not. He doubted the man realized how, in unguarded moments, his expressions played out clearly on his face. Carl wondered what internal struggle his former friend was dealing with, but was determined to stay focused on giving the woman in his arms the attention she deserved. If CeCe had been dealing with Cam's emotional distance the entire time they'd been a couple, Carl could certainly understand her exhaustion.

CeCe's skin felt like wet silk beneath his fingers as he stroked his hands over as much of her as he could reach without moving her out of his arms. He didn't want to do anything that would put space between them, feeling her tightly peaked nipples pressing against his chest was sending every available drop of blood south. He hoped like hell that it was a smooth flight because he wasn't sure his brain was getting enough oxygen-enriched blood to handle the split-second reactions needed to stay balanced on a wet floor if they hit any turbulence. If there was one thing military service had taught him it was to appreciate the luxuries of commercial air travel, and this jet put the first-class seats his parents always insisted on to shame.

Leaning down so his lips brushed over the wet shell of CeCe's ear, "Baby, you are going to be the death of me and we've only just started." He was grateful to hear the small hitch in her breathing as she pressed even closer. "Your body molds against mine and all I can think about is giving your Master the show he's waiting for." He felt her stiffen, "Oh no, he's enjoying what he sees, sweetness, don't doubt that. He wants you to enjoy this moment and judging by his enormous erection, I'd say he is certainly enjoying it. Let's give him something worthwhile to watch."

Carl turned so CeCe's back was pressed against the wall as he started kissing his way down her slender neck and biting down gently on the sweet spot where her shoulder started. Just that small bit of restraint amped up her heart until he could feel her pulse pounding against his cheek. Running his tongue over the mark he'd left, he pressed kisses from one collarbone to the other until he could leave a similar mark on her other side. He ramped things up by pushing her arms behind her and shackling her wrists with one of his large hands. Carl never stopped moving his mouth over her slick skin as he kissed and licked his way to her breasts. "Oh, baby, you have the most beautiful breasts. They are fucking perfect, and these peachy nipples turn the most incredible shade of rose when you are aroused." Swirling his tongue around her areola, Carl could hardly wait to see her peaked nipples clamped with gold chain swinging freely between the jeweled tips.

"I'm surprised you haven't pierced these lovely nipples, sweetness."

"I'm afraid of needles." Her breathless words caught him by surprise. A surgeon who was afraid of needles? That had to make her life interesting. She'd obviously noticed his amusement at her announcement, "I know, it's really insane. I'm not afraid of using them, but I panic if anyone else even looks at me when holding a syringe."

Carl heard Cam's soft chuckle behind them, "It's true. Dr. Barnes' staff knows never to look at her if they are holding a syringe. She uses a very small core group of medical people in her private practice and they are very careful to avoid traumatizing their boss." Carl didn't miss the amusement in Cam's voice and judging by the small furrow between her brows, CeCe hadn't either.

"Magnets perhaps? Those nipple and clit pieces might make you reconsider your needle aversion." Carl wasn't joking. As she would quickly discover the magnetic clamps could be brutal, most were far stronger than anyone realized. The quick pain of piercing would probably be a welcome relief. He felt her shiver against him—*perfect*.

Carl continued his decent pressing kisses against her abdomen. He was pleased when he felt the goose flesh that followed her shudder, he was pleased to know she was as affected by the contact as he was. Feeling the small chill bumps race over her skin urged him closer to her sex. He could already smell the musky scent of her arousal and he could hardly wait to taste her. Carl wanted to feel her honey coating his tongue as he fucked it in out of her channel. He planned to spend hours worshipping her body, but he didn't have the luxury of time now. The water was already starting to cool so it was time to get this show on the road. No doubt he and Cam would be taking icy showers but it would be worth it, and the woman pressing herself against his face needed and deserved this orgasm.

Holding his hand to the side, Carl gave the military's hand sign for *now* and heard Cam respond immediately. "Come for us, pet. Right *now.*" Carl felt her muscles seize before Cam had even finished speaking. He was glad he'd already secured her against the tiled wall because he felt her knees fold but he wasn't willing to let her go until he'd finished lapping every bit of syrup from her sex. "Fuck that is sexy. Watching the flush move over your skin as you come, the changes in your facial expressions—you are so very beautiful, pet."

Carl turned and kissed the inside of both thighs right on the crease between her flowered pussy lips and her legs before biting down ever so gently. "Beautiful and so very responsive. You honor your Master and yourself, sweetness." Standing, he turned and moved her into Cam's arms and quickly washed up before stepping out of the now tepid water. Holding a towel open for her, Carl helped her step out of the shower. By the time he'd dried her, Cam had finished and joined them in the bedroom.

They managed to keep CeCe naked and in between them for the duration of the trip. Carl wasn't sure she'd be able to walk off the jet on her own by the time they landed—hell, he wasn't entirely sure he could. But one look out the windows as they descended was motivation enough. He'd forgotten how much he missed the Caribbean. Brilliant blue water, palm trees, white sand beaches, and brightly painted buildings were just a few of the things he'd fallen in love with the first time he'd accompanied his parents on a holiday to the islands.

As an adult, he appreciated the people—their laid-back approach to life had annoyed him as a teen, but now that he understood the importance of living life in the moment. He was looking forward to the slower pace. Carl felt his chest squeeze at the realization that he'd essentially "thought" himself into the answer. He'd been wondering if he should stay on after this mission was complete, the conversation he'd had with Cam while CeCe slept had been enlightening. Hearing that Cameron Barnes was considering selling Dark Desires to the Wests had surprised him, but Cam's confession that he wanted to become a part-time operative with the Prairie Winds team had floored him. Most of the men joining the Wests' team were single and when they married, it seemed Kent and Kyle managed to arrange for either one or the other to stay home while the other went on missions that involved being away from home for extended periods of time. Ordinarily the assignments the married operatives got were as treacherous, but usually for shorter periods of time. Maybe he'd been shocked because he really couldn't understand why Cameron would even consider *voluntarily* putting himself on a team where he'd be away from his family. *Maybe he'd already been planning to bring in a third? If so, he'll find someone else if I don't stay.* Something about that didn't set well with Carl—not well at all.

CRAIG HAD WATCHED as the group of vehicles pulled out of the parking garage. He almost laughed when he saw the number of decoys they sent in different directions. He didn't doubt they'd be meeting up again a few miles from here, but it didn't really matter since he already knew where they were headed. *Sometimes I even impress myself.*

Turning on his heel he walked happily down the street.

He had plenty of time to make his flight. He'd be staying just down the beach from Cameron's newly rebuilt home. He'd been monitoring all the Barnes' properties for years and the recent remodeling of the beach house had been a dead giveaway they'd be heading there for their upcoming vacation. Listening in on Cameron's phone conversations recently had only confirmed his suspicion. Stopping along the dark sidewalk, he frowned. He would be more excited about the prospect of Cameron and Dr. Barnes moving to the island if he wasn't becoming suspicious that Carl Phillips might be trying to worm his way in—again. Shrugging off his concern, he started whistling softly as he walked. He'd just take care of Carl, too—then there wouldn't be any obstacles.

It wouldn't take long to catch the lovely Dr. Barnes alone on the beach. He'd heard her talk to the other submissives at Dark Desires about how much she was looking forward to sitting out on the beach in the early morning light. She'd had a soft gleam in her eyes when she'd told them how much she loved the few minutes of solitude she found in those early mornings sitting quietly at the water's edge. Oh yes, she was going to be easy to remove from the equation. And once she was gone, Carl would be easy and his death would be inconsequential. In the end, Cameron would only find solace in Craig's arms, and he'd finally realize his true love had been right under his nose all along.

All those doctors his parents had forced him to go to for so many years—they'd all said the same thing. He'd grown so tired of listening to them drone on and on about how you couldn't make someone love you. Craig intended to prove every one of those quacks wrong. He'd eventually stopped going to the appointments his parents made for him, why bother when he had known how wrong all those doctors were. Craig had known the truth since that night at St. Andrew's School for Young Men so many years ago. It was possible to make someone love you, all you have to do is remove their distractions.

Chapter Sixteen

CeCe stepped off the jet dressed in a short tank dress and flip-flops, pausing at the top of the short stairway to take a deep breath and letting the warmth of the sunshine and light ocean breeze warm her skin. The salty air danced over her senses and she sighed in relief. She loved the island, even though she'd been born and raised as a mainlander, she felt most at home here. The small airport was busy and the heavy drums of island music drowned out the soft beating rhythm of the ocean as it pounded against the rock shore, but she still felt the pulse of nature beating inside her. CeCe found herself walking to the beat of the steel barrel drums she could hear in the distance. She'd fallen in love with the music of the islands the first time she and Cam had visited. She'd always believed the island's culture was closely linked to its music, and the vibrancy of the music was definitely a reflection of the friendly people she'd met here. The entire island seemed to pulse in time with the pounding rhythm of the drums as if the power of the ancients was still being sounded hundreds of years later.

Her Masters' presence surrounded her and CeCe was reminded that this trip wasn't going to be like the other relaxed vacations she'd enjoyed here. She faltered at the realization her mind was already beginning to consider Carl Phillips as "hers." *When did that happen? Well, geez,*

Cecelia, perhaps when he had his cock shoved to the back of your throat as Cam pounded into your pussy? Or maybe it was when his hand was swatting you this morning for trying to put on a thong. She was accustomed to being naked at home, but the idea of walking through Customs without panties had almost sent her into a panic. Carl had listened as she'd explained her fears, tucked the thong into his pocket, and proceeded to push back her rising terror by pulling her over his knees, flipping up her skirt and spanking her until the only thing she was thinking about was how much she wanted to come. He'd run his fingers through her labia and praised her when he'd found her slick with arousal. His calloused fingers had teased her to the point she had been convinced a puff of air would have been enough to send her over, but he'd already learned how to read her body too well. Keeping her on edge for several minutes, CeCe had started to worry she'd leave a dark spot on his jeans before they were through. *Nope, nothing embarrassing about that.* When he finally plunged his fingers in and zeroed in on her G-spot without letting up, she felt like she'd been launched into outer space without benefit of a rocket. The orgasm he'd given her had been so strong she still felt a bit unsteady on her feet. Yes, it was official, the two of them were going to kill her with sex. *I can see the headlines back in Houston now...Local surgeon dies while on vacation—Death by Orgasm Details on Page Six.*

Walking through the small airport terminal, CeCe felt the hair on the back of her neck stand straight up, the feeling that she was being stalked was so overwhelming that she stumbled. Cameron and Carl had been close along either side and immediately closed in until there wasn't an inch between them. "Pet? Are you alright?" CeCe had learned early in her relationship with Cameron Barnes that he was always her Master, occasionally he was Master and husband, but he was always her Master first and foremost. She could hear the concern in his voice, but she also knew it was him simply being a Dom—she was his property and he protected and cared for what belonged to him.

"Baby, you need to answer that question before we have another problem to deal with." Carl's words, on the other hand, were laced with the concern of a lover. Oh, she didn't doubt for a minute that he was a Dom. Hell, he oozed alpha male from his every pore, but there was a distinct difference between the two men, and she could practically feel it. One had known love and compassion as a child and the other had not. As a physician dealing with children and young adults, CeCe had seen it a thousand times. There were times she wished she'd become a general practitioner or specialized in pediatrics, perhaps then she could have an impact on the lives of kids by encouraging parents to *hug* their kids every day. The power of positive touch just could not be overstated.

"I'm being watched. I can feel it." The words had no sooner crossed her lips than she felt each of them grasp an elbow and lift her off her feet. Before her mind caught up, they were sprinting toward the exit. It seemed so surreal, the whole terminal seemed to have been frozen in time. The musicians stopped in the middle of a song, people ceased their conversations—no one moved. The scene might have been funny if she hadn't felt the anxiety coming off both Cam and Carl in waves.

CeCe was grateful they hadn't scoffed at her words. So many people thought that just because a woman was submissive, she was a doormat. She didn't even want to think about the number of times someone had said, "I can't believe someone as intelligent as you are would be willing to let a man boss you around like that." What they didn't understand was how freeing submission could be, nor did they seem to grasp how amazing it felt to be protected and cherished above all else. Real Doms don't *boss*, they guide and nurture. The truth was that most of the submissives CeCe knew were incredibly intelligent men and women with colorful personalities and very full social lives. The hardest part about being a sub was learning to look beyond the social stereotypes and accept yourself.

Just as Cam and Carl pushed her into the backseat of the car waiting at the curb, CeCe caught a glimpse of a man who looked vaguely familiar. But he seemed to be focused on following a beautiful blonde woman into a waiting cab parked in front of them making it seem unlikely he'd been watching her so she didn't mention it. Perhaps if she could figure out who he reminded her of—before she could finish the thought Cam turned to her, and in a voice she recognized too well, simply said, "Strip."

LARA STOOD IN front of the enormous windows lining the living room of the Barnes' penthouse looking out over the twinkling lights of boats anchored in Galveston Bay. *Does anyone ever tire of a view this spectacular?* She'd traveled the world with her parents, but missionaries didn't have luxury accommodations. Running water *inside* the hut or screens on the windows would have been considered luxuries in most of the places they'd lived. She smiled when she remembered the look of horror on Peter Weston's face as his brother described the neighborhood where she'd rented an apartment. The tiny studio wasn't in the best part of town, but it was close to campus and Dark Desires, so Lara had considered it a win-win situation. Fischer had watched her closely as she'd explained her reasoning, it was beyond weird to talk to people who were continually trying to read your mind. Since she tried to be honest with others and herself, Lara decided it really didn't matter.

Fischer had made arrangements for men from Dark Desires to pack up and move her things. It didn't matter that they were her coworkers, it still was a bit disconcerting to think about them touching her underclothes. It wasn't like she had a lot of lace and silk lingerie, in fact she'd be surprised if they didn't raze her about her cotton granny panties. *Damn it all to hell, not everybody has a trust fund or parents willing to sell their souls for money.*

Lara's parents were devoted to their work, they were dedicated to education and to helping others succeed so Lara didn't have any legitimate complaints. *But it sure would have been nice if they had devoted as much time to me as they did to other people's kids. Stop feeling sorry for yourself. It never changes anything, so get busy—the only way to enact a change is to act.* She could almost hear her mother reciting the words in her mind. There were no pity parties when Rita Emmons was around, her father was far more compassionate, but even Larry Emmons bowed to his wife's domineering personality. Shaking off the funk she felt herself falling into, Lara turned and walked straight into Fischer's broad chest. The man was like an immovable wall of warmth and her first instinct was to back away, but her second was to press closer.

Realizing what she'd done, the small part of Lara's brain that still recognized the need to protect her heart sparked back to life and she stepped back. "Excuse me, Master Fischer. I was just going, ummm, I need to use the powder room." *Holy shit, did he just growl at me?*

Fischer's hand wrapped around her upper arm and he pulled her close then tipped her face up with his other hand. "We need to lay some ground rules, cupcake, before you get yourself into a peck of trouble as my mama used to say." *Probably not a good sign that he's quoting his mother. Can't imagine that being something a Dom finds all that comfortable.* She could have sworn she'd seen his lips curve up ever so slightly but it was gone so fast she wasn't sure. She wondered if she'd spoken out loud and then wanted to slap her hand against her forehead as it dawned on her— she hadn't *needed* to speak aloud. "I don't need to be an empath to know you are lying, cupcake. Christ, Helen Keller would have known you were lying. So let's just rewind a bit. You should remember that lying is a punishable offense and quite frankly, it's insulting. It is also beneath you."

Damn, that was a low blow. *I may not have much, but I've always prided myself on being true to myself.* "I was going upstairs to be alone for a bit, I'm just trying to take in how much everything has changed." She paused because she really didn't know what else to say without sounding like a sap. When his fingers flexed against her bare skin, it occurred to her that she'd rarely seen Fischer touch anyone. "You're touching me." *Brilliant, Lara. Way to state the obvious.*

"I am. You are one of the few people my brother and I cannot hear from a distance. As it turns out, I can hear scattered bits when I'm touching you. Peter merely feels your emotions with touch. It remains to be seen if our connection strengthens as we get to know each other." *They plan to get to know me? Why? I thought they were just here to guard the place and make sure CeCe's stalker wasn't too nearsighted to tell us apart.*

"Just to be clear, cupcake, Peter and I are here for more than just your protection."

"That's right." Lara jumped at the sound of Peter's voice. She hadn't heard him step into the room, but that wasn't a surprise. From what she'd read about Special Forces soldiers, they could move about in virtual silence. She had noticed Master Cameron moved so stealthily he often startled the subs at Dark Desires, so it stood to reason Peter Weston would do the same thing. *Something to remember.* The man had a smile that Lara was sure made women's knees weak and their panties fall off, why on earth were he and Fischer interested in getting to know her? *Because they can't hear you. You are a novelty, a puzzle to be solved. Tobi said Peter Weston was some sort of puzzle master, so he wants to know why he can't hear all the babbling going on between my ears. Once he figures it out, he'll be gone, just like everyone else.*

PETER REGULARLY CURSED his gifts, being able to *hear* what people were thinking was a far greater challenge than most people understood. But he was quickly coming to see that not knowing what was going through Lara's mind made it impossible to know what to say to her. The sadness he'd seen float through her eyes like a dark storm cloud confused him, but until he'd gotten to know her better, he was just going to have to tread carefully. His mind link with Fischer was helping, but it would be distracting for both of them and he doubted they'd be able to hide that from Lara for long—she was far too perceptive to miss the fact they could communicate telepathically.

Lara's gaze skittered between Peter and Fischer several

times before she focused on Fischer, "Why? Not to be rude, but I've known you for quite a while and you have made it crystal clear you aren't interested in me. So what's changed?" Peter was glad her attention was focused on his younger brother, it saved him the trouble of covering up his smile. She really was amazing—beautiful and smart, but with enough sass to keep them on their toes.

"That's an interesting question, brother. Why don't you explain to Lara why you've allowed her to be under the misconception that you didn't want her?" He was frustrated with his brother as well. While he understood his brother's reasoning, Peter also thought Lara had taken Fischer's distance as disinterest when in fact the opposite was true.

'We'll settle this on the mat later, but rest assured, dear brother, I intend to kick your ass for throwing me under the bus.' Peter watched as Fischer settled Lara next to him on the sofa. "My brother wants me to think he disagrees with my decision to keep my distance, but I promise you he'd be going fucking ape-shit if I hadn't." Peter watched as Fischer drew small circles in the palm of Lara's hand, he wasn't sure whether Fischer was trying to soothe himself or the blonde beauty seated next to him.

"What my brother is trying to spit out is that we intend to share. And without going into a lot of detail, let's just say that we see the fact we can neither one read you at any distance as a sign. A sign that we should spend some quality time with you and get to know you better. Do you have any objection to that?" Peter hated the fact he'd made it sound like some sort of weird business merger, but he'd gotten the impression she was smart enough to understand his meaning.

"Does this include playing at the club? Because that

might be hard for Fischer." Her voice sounded far too insecure for his comfort.

"What do you mean 'hard for Fischer'?" He had the uncomfortable feeling his brother's *distance* was going to come back and bite them in the ass for a long time.

Peter watched as her eyes went glassy with unshed tears. Fischer had been sitting quietly to the side but he'd never taken his hands off Lara's wrist and hand. His brother's jaw tightened and then he broke, "Fuck me. I never meant to hurt your feelings, baby. In fact, I was trying to spare you. There was never any question about me wanting you. Christ, I've spent months trying to hide hard-ons."

When a lone tear slipped free and trailed down her flushed cheek, Peter did what he'd sworn he wouldn't do, he stalked forward and pulled her to her feet. Her hair fell in soft golden waves over his hands as he gripped her shoulders. The silky mass reflected the soft light of the room and made her look like an angel. The first moment he'd seen her, Peter had wondered what it would feel like to have those soft curls brushing over his thighs as she sucked him. Before they played in the dungeon he'd braid her hair so it didn't get tangled in the equipment. He could hardly wait to see her surprise at his braiding skill. *Thank heaven for nieces and young cousins with long hair.*

"We both want you...probably more than we should, but there you have it. We were going to try to go slow. We wanted you to get to know us and I have some catching up to do." Looking down into her face, Peter felt his chest squeeze. *God she is stunning.* He'd been with his share of beautiful women, but it was a miracle Lara Emmons hadn't been snatched up by some modeling scout. Once she was theirs, no one would exploit her beauty for financial gain.

He tamped down his desire to wrap her in cotton and shield her from the world, she was an adult woman who had traveled the world. She'd lived in some of the poorest countries of the world and survived without their coddling, she'd no doubt survive until they could convince her to stay with them. Peter took a deep breath, the unmistakable musk of her arousal surrounded them. Just as he realized he was touching her, a pounding wave of desire washed through him as he watched her eyes dilate. He wasn't sure if the desire was his or hers, but he knew she was theirs in that moment. When she opened her mouth to speak, Peter sealed his lips against hers in a kiss filled with promises of scorching sex and quiet moonlit walks along the beach. The reasoning part of his brain shut down and his impatient inner two-year-old took over without missing a beat. *Mine—Mine—Mine!*

Chapter Seventeen

Kneeling naked on the floor of a moving car isn't as easy as it sounds and CeCe wasn't noticing a lot of concern from the two Masters sitting on either side of her. For the first time since Master C had collared her in the middle of the Dark Desires main lounge, CeCe wanted to curse at him for his unreasonable command. What on earth was his plan? Why did she have to hide on the floor—naked? She hadn't been to the island in over a year and she was being cheated out of seeing the sights along the small coastal highway leading to their small cottage. Sure it was quickly becoming dark and Thomas had seen her naked plenty of other times, but she had been looking forward to seeing the water lapping at the beach as the full moon rose over the water. But most of all she had no idea why she was being punished. *What could I have done to make him so angry?*

She felt a tear splash on to her bare thigh and realized the conversation between the two men had ceased. "Pet?" When she raised her eyes to meet his, CeCe was surprised to see his puzzled expression. "Why are you crying?" *Is he serious? I just don't want to do this all the time anymore.* The sudden realization rocked her to the very foundation of her soul and the sob that emerged from her caused her Master's look of concern to shift quickly to panic. "What the fuck?" She didn't understand the meltdown either, but his response hadn't helped her that was for sure.

"Christ, for somebody so smart you can be really dim sometimes." CeCe turned to Master Carl as he spoke and saw him reaching for a soft throw she hadn't noticed earlier. He wrapped it around her shoulders. He leaned down and picked her up as if she weighed nothing at all and set her on his lap. When he pulled a soft cotton handkerchief from his pocket and dabbed her face, CeCe sobbed so hard he finally gave up and simply cuddled her against his chest. "Just let it all out, sweetness. Holding in all that stress always cycles back, you know, not to mention, as a doctor, you know exactly how bad it is for your health. Adding all that to the side effects of your concussion, hell, it's a wonder you aren't homicidal."

The problem was, CeCe had gotten so accustomed to taking care of those around her that she didn't even know what she liked or needed anymore. She'd just started to realize how narrow her life had become when her Master suggested this trip. Pinning so much on one vacation had been a dumb idea, but it had still happened. When she raised her watery gaze to her Master, he was looking at her with a stern look that caused her to involuntarily wince. His curse sent a fresh wave of tears down her burning cheeks.

CeCe's softly muttered apology was met with a snarled, "What are you apologizing for exactly, pet? For being unhappy and not speaking up? For not taking care of yourself to the point you are so fragile I'm actually considering hospitalizing you? Or for choosing a Master that is such an idiot he ignored a thousand signs that should have told him how unhappy you have been?"

His words hit her like a slap. He sounded so angry and far too close to a "release" for her peace of mind. Sure they were legally married, but everyone she knew living the BDSM lifestyle considered a collar much more binding than a wedding ring. "No. Please. Don't." She heard the pleading desperation in her voice and choked on the racking sobs that tore through her and she pressed her hands over her collar as if she could keep him from unlocking it.

"What the hell?"

"Just don't say anything more. Let me deal with her. I'll get her calmed down. My guess is that she thought you were punishing her by making her kneel naked on the floor. She's been through a lot and from what I've heard, she was already coming from a pretty tenuous place. The only thing about this that really surprises me is that it's taken so long to surface." By the time he'd finished speaking, Carl had pressed kisses to her eyelids and she'd calmed enough she was just hiccupping short sobs. "Close your eyes, baby." When she did, he cuddled her closer, "Breathe with me. I'm not going to count it because I want you to settle enough to feel when I'm taking a deep breath and letting it out." CeCe concentrated on synchronizing her breathing to his and in just a few seconds felt the heavy weight of physical and emotional exhaustion draining away. Letting herself slide into a peaceful sleep was the easiest thing she had done in a very long time.

CARL HAD WATCHED as CeCe skated closer and closer to an emotional ledge as they'd driven down the highway and wondered how long Cam was going to let it go on. He remembered hearing her say she was looking forward to seeing the ocean but he hadn't realized she'd be so upset at not being able to look out the car windows. Looking at Cameron Barnes now, no one would believe he was considered one of the best Doms around. The man's reputation as a club owner and trainer were practically legendary, yet he'd made a series of errors tonight that let Carl know just how distracted he was.

"I wanted to surprise her." When Carl didn't respond, Cam went on, "I didn't want her to see the outside of the house as we drove up. I wanted to lift her out of the car and make it a big deal." He ran his hand through his hair in agitation. "Christ, how could I be so blind? It just seems like the harder I try with her the further I push her away."

"Maybe you need to listen more and arrange less." Carl wasn't surprised to see Cam's puzzled expression. "What I'm trying to say is, you need to listen with your heart. Most women, hell, most people in general, will tell you what they *need* if you are just willing to listen. You don't listen to her. You provide for her physically and sexually, but you aren't even in the building when it comes to her emotional needs. I know that submissives are nurturing by nature, hell, they thrive on helping others, but that doesn't mean they *never* have needs of their own."

Turning in to the short drive leading to the beach house, it was easy to see why she'd been disappointed. The moon was full and the waves made the light look as if a million tiny fairies danced along the surface. It was spectacular. He asked the driver to stop and then turning her on his lap so she wouldn't see the house, Carl kissed her awake. "Open those beautiful eyes, sweetness. Take a look." Her eyes fluttered a couple of times before the long lashes managed to stay up. He heard her sharp intake of breath and smiled over her head at Cam. "Looks like every light imp in the Caribbean is here tonight to greet you. See how they are dancing on the water? I'd say they are quite pleased you have returned."

Her eyes never left the window. Her childlike look of wonder sent a lump into his throat. *God, I could fall in love with her so easily.* Who was he kidding, he was already falling for her. He wasn't sure any of this was going to work out, he only knew keeping her safe had to take precedence over everything else. Her softly whispered words brought him back to the moment, "Thank you. Thank you for waking me. I wanted to see this so badly. And it's even more beautiful than I remembered. I can't tell you how many times the memory of the light waltzing across the surface helped me weather a storm. I've told Chloe all about this place. I know she isn't old enough to fully understand or remember my words, but sharing it helped me remember how peaceful it is."

Carl looked over at Cam and wasn't surprised to see the look of adoration and wonder in his eyes. *He's learning.* Carl let her look for several minutes as they compared the lights of various vessels anchored off shore. He smiled at her curiosity and enthusiasm, wondering what she'd been like as a kid. It was easy to see how much she enjoyed learning. *I'll bet she drove her parents to distraction asking questions.* He could picture her as a kid, eyes wide and pink pouty lips open in awe. Whispering close to her ear, he let his lips brush against its warm shell, "Okay, now before we get out I want you to promise you'll do exactly as your Master tells you. He has a surprise for you and I'm hoping we get to play with you tonight. Playing is so much more satisfying than punishing and I'm looking forward to sinking my cock balls-deep in you. I can hardly wait to feel your body clenching me so tight it's just this side of pain as you milk the cum from me—it's the sweetest feeling in the world." It had been so long since he'd been a woman's lover rather than just her Dom for the night, hell, it wasn't even usually for a whole night. He rarely scened with the same woman more than twice because he'd learned the hard way how easily some submissives developed attachments.

Cam slid her off Carl's lap and slanted his mouth over hers in a kiss hot enough Carl felt his own body responding. "Close your eyes, pet. Don't open them until I tell you. I have been dying to show you this gift." Carl watched as his friend carried his lovely slave to the top of the sandy beach and lowered her bare feet on to the warm sand. Both men chuckled when she sighed and curled her bare toes in the pristine white sand. Turning, Carl glanced at the house, obviously Cam's staff had known they were coming because it looked like every light in the place was blazing brightly. It wasn't as large, but the lights were just as spectacular as Prairie Winds on a club night, particularly one when Tobi had planned something special.

The Prairie Winds Club's specialty shops were being duplicated by almost every exclusive sex club in the country and the concept was quickly spreading outside the U.S. as well. Just last week Carl had sat in the Wests' office and listened in as Tobi and Gracie talked to a group of club owners in Japan. Aside from the obvious language challenges, the cultural differences also came into play. The owners had a difficult time understanding why Kyle allowed his submissive and an employee's sub to speak so "vulgarly" with other men.

Tobi and Gracie had gaped in open-mouth horror at the speakerphone before coming clear up out of their chairs. Tobi West was a tiny little blonde bombshell and seeing her standing with her hands on her hips tapping her foot in frustration made her look like a pissed off Tinkerbell. Gracie had looked over at one of her husbands, "Jax? Would you please explain to these gentlemen that Tobi and I are most certainly not vulgar, we are simply trying to help them with their marketing plan, which wasn't all that impressive when we got it if you want to know the truth." Jax had been leaning against the rock fireplace and winced at her comment.

"Now, Cariño, remember you nor Tobi were as *open* to this sort of thing when you first came here. Remember how embarrassed you were the first time you had to set up a display of anal plugs and lube?" Gracie's cheeks turned scarlet in an instant and she quickly signed something to Jax that made Tobi giggle. Jax and Gracie both had deaf siblings so they often used American Sign Language to communicate privately, but it looked like Tobi was learning as well. *Figures, the little imp is far too nosey to stay out-of-loop for long.* Jax shook his head, "Don't bat those big brown eyes at me, brat. You'll be spending some quality time over my knee this evening for that comment."

Carl had almost laughed out loud when he'd heard Tobi whisper, "Lucky girl." Carl was sure the damned ornery woman had waited until he'd taken a big gulp of coffee before she'd spoken. And Jesus, Joseph, and Mary, that shit had burned coming out his nose.

Shaking off the memory he'd been lost in, he and Cam stood beside CeCe, he smiled at Cam when he realized flanking her had already become second nature for them. The gleam in Cam's eyes let him know his friend understood. "Open your eyes, pet." Carl saw her eyes open and widen as she gasped in surprise. Cam had shown him pictures of the small bungalow before the renovations, so it was easy to understand her surprise. Hell, even the landscaping looked like something you'd see on a home improvement show. *What's the name of that damn show my sister watches? Pimp My Yard? No...oh hell, I don't remember.*

A curving walkway paved with smooth, flat stones with soft lights buried at the surface of the soil illuminated the way to the house. Three large boulders had been placed randomly on the beach and even from this distance, Carl could see embedded anchors for restraints. *Fuck me. Hope we get a chance to test-drive those. We'll give those folks on their fancy boats a show worth breaking out the scopes for.* Carnal images were playing like an old-time movie reel in his head as he watched the moon's soft light illuminate her pale skin. She almost shimmered in the soft golden light and his body responded so strongly he was grateful he'd worn cargo pants, not only had they been comfortable on the plane, they were keeping his cock from bursting out the front zipper of pair of jeans.

Dr. Cecelia Barnes was stunningly, heart-stopping, breath stealing gorgeous. Carl doubted there would have been a single Renaissance master who would have been able to resist capturing her on canvas, preserving images of her beauty for future generations. She was curvy with a natural grace that made her movements so fluid she often looked to Carl like she was floating.

"OH, MASTER, IT'S so beautiful. I can barely believe it's the same house." CeCe knew she'd miss certain things about the quaint home they'd purchased together, but this was a far better version. Even though it was altogether different, he'd also managed to keep some of the original architectural style. "It's amazing, really it is. You've taken a place that was already special and made it truly spectacular. The landscaping is breathtaking and I can't wait to explore it. I can hear the waves lapping at this beautiful beach, but I also hear falling water."

"Yes, love, there is a waterfall along the north side of the house. There is a small, very private all season courtyard just off the new master suite. The wall of our suite retracts so the courtyard becomes a part of the room as well. I think it will be one of your favorite features of the remodel. But I will admit it is actually my second favorite." CeCe recognized Cam's expression and knew from his lust-filled eyes he'd rebuilt the small dungeon. She'd have to be blind to miss the possessive look in his eyes and she wondered if they would actually make it inside before the two of them took her.

CeCe thought she might melt right into the sand, her Master knew how much she loved waterfalls—they calmed her when she was too busy to get to the ocean. She'd had a friend in college who had been into all things New Age and had assured her the reaction was anything but unusual. Pointing out the body's high percentage of water, her friend had explained the connection humans felt to water, but not necessarily the intensity of her own. And once her sweet friend had started talking about "cell memory from previous incarnations" CeCe's attention had drifted back to her black and white world of science. She suddenly realized both men were watching her with a fierce look that made her wonder what she'd missed. "I'm sorry, I got lost for a moment remembering how a friend in college tried to explain the body's connection to moving water. She was nice enough, but a little *out there* if you know what I mean." She realized she was rambling, something that only happened when she was *spent*, so she stopped herself before it got any worse. "Damn it."

She was shocked when she heard Cam's soft laughter, but when she raised her eyes to his, she was surprised to see he was looking at Carl and not at her. "She is very random when she is stressed or overly tired. Since I very much want to watch you fuck her, I am going to go with stressed. Let's go up to the house and see if we can't help her focus a bit." She'd seen the burning hunger in her Master's eyes before, but that had been a smoldering fire compared to the raging inferno consuming them now. *Holy crap on a cottontail, I don't know what he's planning, I hope it doesn't melt me.*

ANCHORED OFF SHORE, Craig Allen watched as Cam led Cecelia and Carl into the beach house. The remodeling had taken so long Craig wondered if the workers were incredibly lazy or if there was more to the project than met the eye. Since he couldn't image Master Cameron tolerating laziness, he was going with the later. Watching them move through large French doors facing the ocean, he tried to imagine himself in Dr. Barnes' place. What would it be like to be sandwiched between Masters' Cameron and Carl? *How would it feel to have one of them pressing his steel shaft between my lips and the other pushing himself into my ass? How would the ridges of Carl's penis feel as they rubbed over my tongue? Would the two of them taste the same? No, I'm sure Cam would taste more rugged, his musk would be more pungent. Carl would taste more subtle, he'd always been smoother than his best friend back in school, so I think he'd have a softer, more natural scent. But I'd make sure I got to taste them both.*

Cameron would push past the tight muscle ring of my ass,

the burn would add so much to the pleasure I'd just barely be able to rasp out the words to beg him not to stop, but of course he wouldn't because I'd belong to him. I'd be caught in a whirlwind of need and arousal. Taking them at the same time—end for end, would be sensual overload. With Carl pressed to the back of my throat and Cameron so deep in my ass his balls would lay atop mine, I'd be close to spontaneously combusting. And then they'd start to move. In and out with soul torturing slow passes designed to ramp up the anticipation for all three of us. They'd both start out whispering what a good boy I was being—the best sub they'd ever had, but soon they'd be shouting how much they wanted to fill me with their cum. And when they both pounded me into a mindless mass of need, Master Cam would lean over and take me in his hand and squeeze. He'd shout for me to come with them and we'd all three go over together before collapsing in a tangled mass of limbs.

His body was reacting to the fantasy as if it was real and leaning against the cushions of the yacht's bow seating was becoming painful. Just as he shifted his weight to give his throbbing erection some much-needed relief, Craig heard the clicking of heels on the boat's wood deck. The annoying sound brought him fully out of the fantasy he'd been enjoying. *Why do women think that click-clacking is attractive? Drives me fucking nuts.* He'd been enjoying his fictional romp with Cameron and Carl so much he'd nearly forgotten his "cover." Sherry had been more than happy to share her taxi at the airport. Craig had known the moment CeCe had *felt* him watching her, he could only hope she hadn't recognized him as they'd gotten into the cab parked in front of the Towne car that met the Barnes. Once he'd been alone with Sherry, it had been easy to convince the brainless blonde to join him on his father's yacht for a few days. *What kind of bimbo agrees to go with a man she doesn't know onto a boat? Dizzy bitch.* "Hey, you didn't forget about me, did you? What are you doing out here anyway? Is that your house?"

Christ, I should just throw her snooping ass overboard now. "No, I was just looking for a beach for us to enjoy tomorrow. That one looks great. We'll take the jet skis over and take a look tomorrow."

She seemed pacified and nodded, "Okay. I have the wine poured and your staff made dinner. Come on, let's eat before we find a way to pass the time under the stars." Had he not noticed in the cab that her voice was annoying? He was going to have to concentrate on not strangling her until she'd served her purpose. Once his parents finally signed over the last of the company's majority shares to him they had no longer served any purpose, so they'd become a liability. It had merely been a tragic coincidence when they died just a couple of months later. Yes, a tragic *coincidence*, indeed. He'd taken over the company and then promptly put his trusted attorney at the helm and left for Houston to win Cam's heart. The man he'd left in charge had been more than happy to send the luxurious boat to St. Maarten if it meant keeping his plumb position a little longer.

"Hey, I'm getting lonely in there all by myself." *Yeah, that whining is good enough reason to drown her.* He got to his feet and followed her inside. He had no intentions of fucking her, but he'd practice his oral skills and make sure she fell asleep in a well-satisfied stupor. A couple of great orgasms and she'd leave him alone for the rest of the night. If things went according to his plan, he'd be able to take care of the illustrious Dr. Barnes tomorrow and hell, maybe Lady Luck would take a shine to him and he'd be able to pin the whole thing on Miss Buxom Bimbo. He'd make nice over dinner then *buy* her loyalty with a couple of mind-blowing releases. Yeah, a couple of scream the walls down orgasms later she wouldn't even notice he hadn't fucked her. Women were great as friends and he didn't mind using them as a means to an end—but they certainly didn't do anything for him sexually.

Chapter Eighteen

Aspen dropped the tiny capsule in Craig's wineglass and watched it bubble for a few seconds before all trace of the sedative disappeared. *That ought to knock his ass out for a few hours. Pissant.* Turning her attention to the man looking through a scope at Cameron and Cecelia Barnes' beach home, she shook her head. How big did his ego have to be in order to think he'd simply "picked her up" in the airport? Hell, she'd been tailing him since New York. Yeah, Kyle and Kent were going to owe her big time for this. But then again, it was colder that fucking Antarctica in New York and the warmth of St. Maarten and a few days of tropical paradise was a sweet way to spend the last of her leave.

She'd known the West boys and Jax McDonald since they'd all been kids in Austin, so she'd been happy to help when they'd called. She hadn't even asked how they'd known she was in New York, she'd just assumed that had been Micah Drake's doing. God, that man was wicked with a computer, she'd heard tales about him for years. Letting him go had been one of the dumbest things Uncle Sam had done in a long time. She hadn't been surprised to learn Micah and Jax were best friends, but she had been surprised to find out the two men now shared a wife and young daughter.

She'd enjoyed playing super spy donning night vision

goggles and laying on the roof of a building just down from the one where her friends had been staying. As a fighter pilot, Aspen didn't get to play soldier on the ground very often, so she'd had fun watching the skinny weasel as he watched from the shadows. *Damn, those goggles were kick-ass.* She'd tapped the small button on the side sending several still shots to Micah back in Austin. He'd recognized the guy from Cameron Barnes' employee files, and was now running him through his face recognition programs. Aspen had no doubt that by the time Micah was done with the jerk laying out on the bow, they'd know everything there was to know about him, including his real name because no one believed the one on his employment information was real. Sighing to herself, she was actually worried this was too easy, because she'd only spent an hour or so with the man and she already knew he had a major hard-on for Cameron Barnes.

Aspen didn't know Cameron Barnes personally, but his reputation was well known in military circles and from what she'd heard recently, that was being eclipsed by his reputation as a BDSM club owner and Master. Part of the bargain she'd struck with Kyle and Kent had been a five-year membership to Prairie Winds. She would still have two years left by the time she was discharged but at least she'd be able to enjoy a few visits a year until she could really take advantage of her new prize. Taking a deep breath before stepping out on to the boat's moonlit deck, Aspen shook her head. So often men were just too easy. Put long, tumbling blond curls, a smile fit for a toothpaste commercial, a bit of Texas twang, and a big set of hooters in front of them and they'd follow you over the edge of the Grand Canyon. *Idiots.* She'd given up looking for a man who could earn her submission by demanding her respect, finding him just seemed too remote of a possibility. But that didn't mean the hot guy she'd seen standing down the block from her target hadn't been worth checking out. She'd known he was part of the Prairie Winds' team, but hadn't been introduced to him since she'd been pulled in to pinch-hit at the last minute. She'd finally gotten Jax to tell her his name right after they'd landed in St. Maarten—yeah, she'd be looking up Mitch Ames the next time she was in Austin, that was for sure. But right now, it was time to get this show on the road. The sooner Allen drank the wine, the sooner she could snoop around and call Jax. She could only hope to find proof this was their guy so she could get away from Mr. Limpy—*Fuck me he's just plain creepy.*

IT HAD TAKEN Carl and Cam both to keep Cecelia from wandering through the house. Cam wanted her to have something to look forward to tomorrow, but even more than that, he wanted to show her a few of the special features in the courtyard and master bath. After stopping in the master suite to grab a few supplies, Cam watched his sweet woman's face as he pressed buttons on the small remote that had been set on the bedside table just as he'd requested. He heard her small gasp as the entire wall retracted, opening up the large room to the outside paradise. "Come," he commanded as he took her hand and led her forward. The smooth flagstone path wound through the palms and bright tropical flowers to the waterfall. Tonight the underwater lights were all soft blue and white, but Cam knew they could be changed to suit any mood. With another touch to the remote, music came from the hidden speakers and he saw her expression soften as she recognized the gentle piano music of Brian Crain.

Turning her so she noticed the retracting wall also opened up the master bath's shower area, Cam watched her eyes widen in recognition. "How did you know?"

"Pet, it's my job to know what your heart desires, even when you don't voice those desires. Especially when you don't voice them." He didn't say any more, now wasn't the time for that discussion.

Without speaking, he moved her into position beside a large boulder, pressing gently between her shoulder blades to lean her over the rock's curved side. Pulling silk scarves from his pocket, Cam wrapped her wrists and then secured each of them to small handholds just over the top of the stone. Turning to Carl, he glanced down at her ankles and handed the man the other two silk scarves. Stepping back, Cam watched as Carl moved to behind Cecelia and began stroking his hands up and down her legs as he moved them out further with each pass. Cam stepped to Cecelia's side and began unbuttoning the cuffs of his shirt. Her eyes followed his movements as if she were being hypnotized by them, and even in the dim light Cam could see moisture glistening from her rose-colored lips as she licked them when he unbuttoned the front of his shirt and pulled it from his pants. Tossing it aside, he watched her eyes dilate and begin to cloud with desire. *Perfect.*

Pressing the small remote in his palm, Cam watched as a large three-part video screen lowered from the tall palms on the opposite side of the small koi pond. When the images appeared, he heard Cecelia's small gasp and Carl's muttered, "Fuck that's hot." They hadn't had time to notice the cameras placed around the enclosure, there wasn't a square inch of the area that couldn't be projected on the screen. The security team would also be able to see the area, but they were men well versed in the ways of BDSM play so they weren't going to be shocked by anything they saw. The one feature Micah Drake had insisted Cam include was a program that ensured all videos were stored on a separate server that only Cam had the code to access. He'd still have a recording if there was ever a security issue, but he was the only one with access. In light of the recent threats against his family, Cam was grateful he had heeded his friend's advice.

He'd left his black slacks on but removed his belt so the trousers rode low on his hips as he crossed his arms over his bare chest and watched his pet slide further and further into the correct mindset. Cam understood this part of her personality and could interpret even the slightest shift in her body's language. He could meet each and every one of her physical needs, it was the emotional components that seemed to elude him. Pushing aside that concern, he focused on her every breath, and watched her pulse beating at the base of her neck, the longer he studied her the faster it became. Her breasts were pressed against the surface of the rock, but he knew from experience her nipples would already be tightly beaded and reaching out for his attention.

When Carl had finished securing her legs, he stood and looked to Cam for further instructions. Both men had been advised one of the club's employees was being investigated as the person who had made the threats, but they hadn't told Cecelia yet. Because they knew the man was anchored close by they wouldn't prolong the exposure, but Cam knew all three of them needed this scene. "Tell me, is our pretty little toy wet for us, Carl?" Cam had deliberately referred to his friend as Carl rather than as Master Carl because he intended to top him as well—the change wasn't missed by either Carl or Cecelia.

Her eyelids fluttered closed for just a few heartbeats as Carl moved his fingers through her soaked pussy lips. Holding his glistening fingers up for Cam to see, he answered, "Yes, Sir, she is indeed." And there is was, the acknowledgment that Carl was ready to play. The words nearly brought Cam to his knees in gratitude.

Tossing a small tube of lube to Carl, Cam watched as he caught it easily without ever moving his gaze from Cam's. "I want to watch your cock slide in and out of her sweet ass." Cecelia's low moan shifted his attention to her. "Pet? Are you angling for a punishment before we even start?"

"No, Sir. I'm sorry, Sir. I wasn't protesting, it just that, well...your words turned me on—a lot and it slipped out." Cam had to bite the inside of his cheek to keep from smiling. *This is one of the down sides of the cameras.* He watched her for a few seconds and then nodded. She let out a breath he was willing to bet she hadn't even realized she'd been holding. *Christ, is she that worried about displeasing me? I want her submission, but I don't want her so worried she'll displease me that she is afraid to show any emotion at all.* For the first time since they had been together, Cam realized he really had grown tired of seeing her role in his life in such narrow terms.

The snap of the cap from the lube bottle opening shifted his attention to Carl. Watching as he spread Cecelia's cheeks apart and dribbled the cool liquid over the pink rosette of her ass sent a flood of blood to Cam's already rock hard cock. Her sweet gasp as the cool gel slid over her hot ass and sex added another layer of lust to the raging need already consuming him. It was going to take every bit of the control he was so well known for to hold himself back, because in this moment the only thing he could think about was pushing himself into Carl's tight ass. Knowing his every thrust was pushing Carl deeper into Cecelia was going to drive him out of his mind once they'd started.

"Tell me how it feels, pet. Do you like knowing I'm watching as Carl prepares you? Does it arouse you to know how much you are pleasing me?" His voice rasped out the questions, but he was pleased he'd been able to form coherent questions when his brain was being starved for oxygen. *If any more blood goes south, I'm not even going to be able to remember my own name.*

"It feels so good…his hands are touching all the right spots and the anticipation is almost more than I can stand. But the best part? Oh…the very best part is knowing you are pleased with me. And seeing it all on the monitors is so hot…just seeing it all is pushing me so close and Master Carl's fingers are stretching me and I want to feel him push inside, but first…" Cecelia's voice had trailed off and a very small sliver of Cam's brain was grateful because her words had been a hair's breadth from blowing his control into tiny bits of vaporized matter. But his curiosity about what she *hadn't said* pulled him back from the brink.

"What? Tell your Master what you want first, pet. You have piqued my curiosity." He was fairly certain he knew what his little voyeur wanted, but he was going to make her say it. He was standing just out of her line of sight but she looked up and met his gaze squarely in the monitor. The wanton look on her flushed face should be in every Dom training manual with the caption, "This is the look you want to see on your submissive's face."

"I want to see you kiss him. I want to see you kiss Carl, make him a part of us." Carl's eyes went molten and Cam was stunned at how perfectly she'd read the situation. He'd hoped to ease her into the idea of a permanent ménage, but she was already right where he'd hoped tonight would take her. Shifting his gaze to Carl's, he quirked a brow in question. The small nod was almost imperceptible, but Cam hadn't missed it.

Cam moved closer to Carl and smoothed his hand down the smooth skin of Cecelia's ass without ever breaking eye contact with Carl. "Do you know what we're asking of you?" Carl shifted his eyes down for just a second before raising them again. The acknowledgement of Cam's dominance was unbelievably sexy and he didn't waste another moment before threading his fingers through Carl's shaggy blond hair and sealing their lips together. Cam felt his cock harden even more—something he would have sworn wasn't possible, then Carl opened to his probing and Cam's knees nearly buckled from the pleasure. Carl tasted as good as he had all those years ago, but there was a new strength in his response that hadn't been there before. Cam knew it was indication of Carl's maturity and commitment to what they all three wanted to explore, and it was a fucking turn on.

Cam had become so lost in the feel of Carl's lips against his own, the remarkable way the man tasted, and the heady feeling he got from dominating the only man he'd ever wanted to possess, he'd almost forgotten they were being watched by the woman they both wanted. Cam wasn't sure if it was his own need for oxygen or Cecelia's quiet, "Holy shit that's hot," that had him pulling back, but the very fragile hold he'd had over his control was dangerously close to snapping.

"Push that beautiful cock of yours into her pretty little asshole. Stretch it, make it burn for you. I want you to take her exactly as I plan to take you." Cam could only hope he'd be able to hold back long enough to make it memorable for the two of them. Using the remote to zoom the camera in close on them, he saw Cecelia's shoulders tense as the large purple domed head of Carl's cock pressed against her puckered opening. "Don't try to keep him out, pet. You are better trained than that. Your Master wants this. Will you deny me this pleasure?" The effect of his words was immediate. Cam watched as her muscles relaxed and she pressed back as much as the restraints allowed, as if seeking Carl's cock. Her back arched perfectly, presenting herself with perfect submission. "Very nice. You make me very proud."

"Jesus Christ, she is already pulsing around me and I'm barely inside her. Her sweet ass is literally pulling me deeper. Fucking amazing." Carl's voice wasn't much above a whisper and Cam wasn't even sure he'd intended to speak out loud.

"She is amazing. And just so you know, she'll be just that remarkable each and every time she gives herself to you. She is more generous than she should be and we will have to work together to ensure she doesn't wear herself out." Cam knew his friend was listening, even though his attention was focused on Cecelia, his hands stroking over her ass cheeks and lower back in loving strokes meant to relax her so she'd allow his penetration without coming herself. Shifting his attention to the large monitors on the other side of the water, Cam watched as Cecelia and Carl's expressions showed the intensity of the moment. *How in the hell am I ever going to get through this? I'm going to blow the moment I'm inside him. The feel of his bare back pressed against my chest is something I've dreamt about since we were yanked apart by the school officials that last night at St. Andrew's.*

Chapter Nineteen

CARL COULDN'T REMEMBER ever being as aroused as he was looking down on CeCe as she arched her back presenting herself to him. He wasn't known as a stickler for protocol, as long as a sub let him take the reins, he wasn't going to fuss at her to keep her back level or her knees a certain width apart. Carl had seen Doms stop a scene over minutia when they should have been so lost in the pleasure they wouldn't care about the little crap. Jesus, who cared if you could lay a fucking fine china tea set on the woman's back—just fuck her already. He'd always wanted to tell them to just let yourself fall into the mind numbing pleasure and chill the fuck out. But looking down on CeCe's perfect form, seeing her flatten her back and feeling how that opened her up to deeper penetration, he was starting to understand their reasoning.

When CeCe had asked Cam to kiss him, Carl's knees had nearly folded. Then to hear her say she wanted him to be a part of their relationship had almost shredded his control. The devastating distraction of Cam's kiss had been the only thing to pull him back. He'd wondered a million times over the years if Cameron Barnes' kisses were really as earth moving as he remembered, and they were. Time has a way of skewing memories, but this once his recollection was point on—the man's kiss was so perfectly balanced between seduction and demand it had completely leveled him.

Wrapping his fist around his cock, Carl wasn't surprised to feel the heated skin, hell, the rest of his body had to be functioning without much blood supply because it was all pooled in his groin. Just touching himself made him groan with need. Pressing the tip against CeCe's ass sent a ripple of arousal through her and Carl watched the small shiver move through her muscles like a small wave. The woman's control was teetering on the edge as well and he was perversely pleased to know he *wasn't* the only one affected.

Cam was talking to them and a small sliver of Carl's brain acknowledged the fact CeCe was responding, but he wasn't able to make out the words over the sound of his own heartbeat pounding in his ears. *Jesus, Joseph, and Mary. She is going to bring me to my knees before I even get her off.* He hadn't come before the woman he was fucking since he'd been a teenager, but if he didn't get his head back in the game, this was going to end far too soon. Looking up at the monitors, Carl watched as the camera zoomed in on his cock pressing in to CeCe's ass. The picture was hot enough to sizzle, but the center screen captured his attention. Seeing the look on CeCe's face as he pushed balls deep into her rectum enthralled him. Her features reminded him of a porcelain doll, a very erotic and hot doll. Her concentration never wavered, but the need was easy to read in her eyes.

Carl closed his eyes for a few seconds and let his mind wrap itself around all the sensations flooding his body. His senses were being bombarded with the scent of CeCe's arousal and the musky smell of naked men overlaying the sweet smell of the night jasmine blooming around them. Carl had shed his clothes as soon as they'd walked into the master suite, he'd never been intimidated by nudity and being naked with CeCe was never going to be a hardship. The look of appreciation he'd seen in her eyes had been a huge ego boost as well. When her body pulsed around his cock as the tight muscles tried to pull him deeper into her heat, he cursed under his breath. *Hell, baby, I can't get any further in you, and you are already stealing my soul.* And then, just as he didn't think he could stand any more, Cam walked up behind him and pressed his muscled chest flat against Carl's back. Feeling Cam's chest hair brushing against his heated back ramped up his need and Carl heard himself groan. Leaning down he slid his hand under her, he was grateful Cam hadn't tied her so tightly he wouldn't have been able to cup her breasts in his hands. He managed to roll the tight tips between his fingers and smiled when she arched into his touch.

Bending forward over CeCe had given Cam the access he needed and Carl heard the sound of the lube bottle being opened just before the cool gel trickled down the crack of his ass. Cam's large finger began massaging the slick gel into the tight ring of muscles surrounding his hole without breaching it as Carl felt Cam lean over him from the side. Looking up at the monitor, he felt the air leave his lungs when he saw the dark demand written in Cam's expression. He intended to take, plunder, and possess—the only question was, would he walk away again like he had so many years ago. "Tell me." Cam's words had been growled against Carl's ear, and he wouldn't pretend he didn't know exactly what the man meant.

"Will you walk away again?" He hadn't meant to say it. He certainly hadn't meant to blurt it out so bluntly. But it was done now, and he'd just have to deal with the consequences.

Cam went still beside him and Carl searched the man's

gaze in the monitors for anger, but only saw regret. "I thought I was doing the right thing. I was trying to spare you the embarrassment I was sure would follow." Carl was convinced that much was true, Cameron Barnes was nothing if not loyal. He had no doubt felt that if claimed he'd been the aggressor, Carl would be seen as a victim. He'd tried to give him an easy out, but Carl had shouldered his share of the blame even though the consequences had been devastating. The pain of that time in his life was compounded by feelings of abandonment, losing his best friend had been the worst part of the nightmare his life became in the blink of an eye. One minute he'd been mindless in the pleasure and the next he'd been alone. During one of his forays into self-destruction, he'd decided perhaps the military would be a great escape. Carl always found it interesting how fate could maneuver you right where you needed to be because that decision—which had been made for all the wrong reasons, had ended up saving his life. Shaking off the bad memories, Carl met Cam's gaze and looked deep into his former friend's eyes. The eyes were the same, yet so very different. There was wisdom and pain that hadn't been there before, but the soul of the man studying him with equal interest was still the same.

"I've never made a decision I regretted more." Cam's words had been spoken softly, but they'd pierced the shield Carl built around his heart after that night. He knew it couldn't be healed overnight, but a new warmth moved through him infusing him with a newfound hope. "I can't promise that this will last forever. Fuck, even traditional couples can't make that promise, even though they try. What I can promise you both is that I'll always be honest with you. I'll never make a decision without having your best interest at heart. And I'll never leave you until we have discussed it—I'll never leave without saying goodbye."

Carl nodded once, letting Cam know he was satisfied with his answer, and when he looked down at CeCe his heart clenched at the tear tracks on her cheeks. "Baby, don't cry, you'll break my heart."

She smiled sweetly and said, "It's okay, they are tears of joy, not pain." Then her indulgent smile turned naughty, "Although, I'm awfully close to dying of need. Can we get on with this, because I can't even tell you how much I want to see my Master fuck you while you fuck me."

"There's a nice punishment session in your future, pet. Topping from the bottom is not going to be tolerated, no matter how much I agree with you." Carl knew by the look in Cam's eyes, CeCe's punishment wasn't going to be anything she wouldn't enjoy, probably more than she should. *And damn it all to hell if I'm not actually looking forward to seeing a few of my own handprints on that lush ass of hers. I hope like hell she likes what Cam has to show her tomorrow because I wouldn't have any trouble getting used to living here.*

CAMERON HADN'T EXPECTED Carl's blunt response, but he hadn't been entirely blindsided either. He could honestly say he was relieved to have finally discussed the elephant in the corner. Cam could only hope that since it had finally been brought up, they'd be able to move on. There was so much more for them to work on, he didn't want to get hung up on this. Cam had also known exactly what Cecelia had been doing when she'd mentioned getting on with it, the little imp hadn't been topping from the bottom at all; she had simply been trying to lighten the mood, and her "punishment" was going to look an awful lot like a reward.

Grabbing a nearby hand towel, he spoke to Carl as he dried his hands, "Fuck her slowly. I want to watch while I undress. I don't want either of you to come until I'm there with you." He had to hold back his smile when both Cecelia and Carl groaned as Carl slowly withdrew from her tight hole. Cam took his time removing his clothing, not that he'd left much on, but simply because the scene in front of him stole every bit of his attention. Listening to Carl's soft murmurings as he praised Cecelia was ramping up his arousal even though he was merely an observer. But watching Carl's hard cock disappear into Cecelia made him impatient to see his own throbbing member disappearing into Carl.

Drizzling more lube into Carl's crack and then pushing against the tight ring until his fingers met resistance made him growl. "Don't try to keep me out. Your body remembers how to do this. Most important, it remembers how incredible it feels when I'm all the way in. The only thing better? That sweet slide in and out, shocking all those neglected nerve endings to life until the cum in your balls boils out of control sending lightning up your spine. You'll come deep in our sub's ass when I'm filling yours. Now, press out and let me prepare you."

The next few minutes seemed to drag even though he enjoyed the power he felt dominating both Carl and Cecelia. Knowing they were both submitting to him, letting him direct their pleasure, was a heady feeling. He would reward their trust in ways they couldn't even yet imagine. He had always cherished Cecelia's submission above all else. Cam loved his daughter with all his heart, but he knew her soul wasn't his to keep. His role was to provide for her, love her, and help her find her way in the world. The goal was to let her go with as much preparation as possible, but in the end, she'd have to follow her own path. But, Cecelia was his to nurture and protect until death separated them. Even if she decided to leave him tomorrow, Cam would always provide for her and ensure her life was as worry-free as possible.

Cam made sure he stepped out so the camera would show him clearly as he squirted lube into his own hand and then wrapped his fingers around his cock. Carl leaned forward and spoke against Cecelia's ear, "Do you see that, baby? That is all for us, Master Cam is more than a little aroused by our little show here. Just think how incredible it's going to be when each thrust he makes into me pushes me into you. It's going to be a chain reaction. Think nuclear fission, totally out of control and explosive once it's set into motion. But fuck, baby, it's going to send us all into an orgasmic coma, mark my word." Cam couldn't have agreed more, but didn't comment. The moment had been intimate between the two of them and Cam wanted them to build on the bond they'd already formed. It wasn't easy to step back, but he was determined to do whatever was required to insure his sweet wife's happiness.

Moving so he was standing behind Carl, Cam adjusted the cameras and then set the remote to the side. He wanted to be able to enjoy the images, but even more, he wanted to have both hands free to touch the man bending over in front of him. Stroking himself in a tight fist, Cam enjoyed the slick feel of the lube as it warmed under his touch. Spreading his feet apart, he stepped closer and pressed the tip against Carl's hole. "Your bodies are mine to enjoy. Pet, your body belongs to both of us, but Carl's is mine alone to pleasure when we are playing." As he pressed through the tight muscles, Cam had to catch his breath as the pleasure washed over him. *Holy fucking hell, I'm never going to last.* "That's not to say I may not direct his pleasure, but it's still mine to provide when we are playing." He'd managed to keep talking while pressing forward but it had nearly drained his control.

Carl's muscles flexed around him and Cam growled in response, "Jesus, we have to do this or I'm going to lose the last shred of finesse I'm holding on to."

"Yes. Come on, sweetness, let's chase it." Carl's words were evidently all it took for Cecelia to let go. Watching her expression in the monitor, Cam saw her eyes glaze over and knew she was lost in the passion. God he loved seeing that look in her eyes—knowing he'd had a part in giving her that kind of pleasure was heady stuff, indeed. Cam began thrusting in and out of Carl's hot ass in synch with Carl's own measured thrust into Cecelia. "Your body is made for this, baby. You are so responsive, your body is burning me alive." Cam couldn't remember ever hearing Carl Phillips' voice sound as deep and raspy as it did now, and it was one of the sexiest things he'd ever heard. If the man walked away from them, Cam wasn't sure he'd survive it, and the stark truth of what he'd done all those years ago hit him like a ton of bricks. Leaning forward, he pressed a kiss between Carl's shoulder blades and whispered an apology that was long overdue.

Looking up at the monitor one last time, Cam wanted to shout out his joy for everyone to hear. He finally had everything he'd dreamed of within his grasp and in this moment his life was as close to perfect as it had ever been. Before he could get lost thinking about tomorrow, he pulled his mind back, determined to enjoy *this moment*. Just as it should be, Cecelia came first, her scream was probably echoing off the nearby rock cliffs. In the back of Cam's mind, he wondered if they'd be getting a visit from the local constable. But the thought was lost in the next instant when Carl's arm snaked back to wrap around Cam's hip locking the two of them together. The move might have been lust driven, but its significance wasn't lost on Cameron. The next second both men shouted their release as Carl's muscles locked down like a vise wringing the last drop of cum from Cam's cock.

Cameron saw black spots dancing in front of his eyes when his brain came back on-line and he was grateful he'd locked his knees—passing out and collapsing from an orgasm probably violated some part of the Dom-code. Hell, he'd probably have to turn in his card or something. *Goddammit, I'm thinking like a fucking wimp. But shit, I'm damned lucky that didn't fry all my brain cells. I'm lucky I can think at all.* "As soon as my legs work, we'll take a shower and then rest. But that may be a while—right now I can't feel my hands or feet. Fuck me, that was amazing."

Cam heard Carl's grunted agreement, but when he looked up at the screen, Cecelia's eyes were closed. "Pet? Shit, is she okay?"

"Yeah, just passed out. I can feel her breathing, but she is certainly in need of some aftercare." Carl's voice was full of tenderness as they both moved to disentangle themselves and release Cecelia from the restraints. As they rubbed her arms and legs to ease the muscle strain her dark lashes fluttered and finally rose. Cam saw a whole new look of love in her eyes and then as if they'd rehearsed it, he and Carl both leaned down and kissed her temple before Cam picked her up in his arms and they all three made their way back inside.

"She humbles me. I have done so many horrible things in my life—granted I was doing them for what I was convinced were noble reasons, but it doesn't change the fact I've ended a lot of lives and I feel each of those as if it were a black mark on my soul. But I've obviously done some things right, because she is a blessing I never expected fate to send me." Cam watched as Carl started filling water in the enormous bathtub and added the healing salts that had been set out for them. "Chloe is another gift, and one neither Cecelia nor I have been able to spend enough time with. She deserves better than we've given her, and my hope is that if you stay, the three of us will be better parents than two."

Settling in the warm water with his cuddly pet cradled on his lap, Cam met Carl's gaze in the mirrors surrounding the tub and saw the question in his eyes. "There isn't anything I won't share with you if you'll devote yourself to our family. If it's mine to give, you'll have it. I want us to both be free to help with the teams when we can, but we won't ever be gone at the same time. We'll never work on the same missions either, that way our family will always have one of us to rely on."

He looked down to see Cecelia's were open and she was studying him closely. "Thank you—for giving me what I didn't even know I wanted. But more importantly, thank you both for having the courage to try. I really believe you have needed this as well." When she reached out her hand, Carl wrapped both of his around her much smaller one before scooting closer.

"Beautiful and brilliant. We are blessed, brother." Carl's quiet words of acceptance filled Cam's heart with hope that everything he'd set in place was going to work out perfectly. *Now, if Captain Andrews can just get the goods on Allen before he hurts anyone, and Cecelia falls in love with the clinic, we can start our new life here.*

Chapter Twenty

Aspen watched as Craig Allen struggled to stay awake and couldn't help but be a little bit impressed with his valiant, but doomed, efforts. When Mitch had given her the small capsules, he'd assured her that one was plenty for a man of Allen's height and weight. He'd also stressed the drug would kick in slowly so it wasn't obvious to the victim he or she had been poisoned. *Yes, I can certainly see where that little detail is significant, especially in light of the fact I may still be here when he wakes up.*

To be honest, she was really starting to worry that the stuff wasn't ever going to kick in enough to take his creepy ass down. *Shit, maybe I should have used both caps.* Knowing her luck, she'd have killed him. Sighing to herself, she tuned out his drugged rambling and considered how hard it would be to explain to her commanding officer that she'd killed a civilian who was *suspected* of stalking the legendary Cameron Barnes. Christ, the man was a hero legend among Special Forces operatives—didn't seem likely her C.O. would believe that Barnes would have needed her help. Might be easier to just disappear for the next five or six decades. She wouldn't have any trouble hiding from the government, but there wouldn't be a corner of the world dark enough or a hole deep enough to escape the eagle eyes of Micah Drake.

When Allen finally admitted he was done for the night

and retired to his cabin, Aspen got busy searching the yacht. She'd been concerned when the crew had lingered after serving dinner, but they'd scattered as soon as dessert had been served. When he'd heard the outboard motor on the small transport fire up, Allen had waved it off saying he'd given the crew the night off so they would have some privacy. *Ewww, just kill me now.* The idea of needing privacy with him was enough to make her toss back up the dinner she'd just barely touched. It hadn't seemed wise to risk having him drug her as she'd done him.

After watching to be sure he'd made it to his stateroom, Aspen had checked the satellite phone the team had given her. Not finding any messages indicated the team had miraculously solved the case since their last communication, she set to work after switching on the small device Jax had assured her would scramble any security cameras on board. *No need to record my snooping for posterity.* Even though she was an expert swimmer, the idea Allen could take her several miles further off shore and then toss her overboard didn't set well. Sure, she had the tracking device the team had given her, but it would still take time for them to scramble a rescue unit and becoming shark bait was actually pretty low on her bucket list—it was above being a guest for any of the major terrorist fractions, but just barely.

By the time she heard the whine of the outboard returning, the sun was starting to peak over the horizon and Aspen was dead on her feet. She'd searched the entire boat and hadn't found anything relating to Cameron Barnes. The one thing she'd found that seemed completely out of place was an old high school yearbook from a boys' school in update New York. She hadn't taken time to look through it, but she had snapped a picture of it and sent it in because something about it had seemed so out of place in the otherwise immaculate office. She'd barely had time to return to her smaller stateroom and turn off the scrambler before taking the world's fastest shower and falling into bed. *Hopefully he'll sleep for a couple more hours and I can catch a few myself before he decides to check out the beach.*

CECE FOLLOWED CAM into the small clinic that was only about a mile from their home and smiled at the patients waiting to be seen by a member of the medical office's small staff. The place was remarkably clean and smelled like fresh paint. She wasn't a fool, she'd known from the moment Cam had suggested they check it out that something was amiss. The elderly doctor who greeted them had obviously been expecting them because he'd been standing beside the receptionist's small desk.

After the "oh-so-polite" introductions, CeCe looked around the small waiting room while Cameron and Carl talked to the head of the clinic. She was listening with half-hearted interest—lost in taking in the number of children with crudely made crutches laying alongside their chairs or sitting in wheelchairs. Their small faces focused on her, hope dancing in their bright eyes. Turning to the doctor, she didn't even wait for the men to stop speaking, "Tell me."

Dr. Guzman didn't pretend he didn't understand her question, he simply led her around the small waiting room quietly introducing her to each child and briefly explaining his or her condition. CeCe was amazed at how candidly he spoke and he'd evidently noticed her response, "We do not have HIPPA here in St. Maarten, Dr. Barnes. You will find there are very few secrets on this small island and whether you consider that a blessing or a curse usually depends on whether or not you are behaving yourself, isn't that right, children?" CeCe couldn't hold back her laughter as all their heads nodded.

There were several children who could be walking within hours with the proper surgical intervention, and the rest could be mobile within a few months. "Don't you have a surgeon on staff at the hospital? Maybe someone to fly over from another island to work a day or two a week?"

"No. Patients have to fly to the doctor and as you can imagine the costs are prohibitive for most of our population."

While Dr. Guzman's words had saddened her, the tears of one mother had broken her heart. Her dark eyes were silently beseeching CeCe to help while she cradled a small boy in her lap. The young mother was quietly rubbing his twisted leg and CeCe wondered if it was to comfort her or her young son. "I wish my license allowed me to help them. In a few hours I could do a lot." She hadn't really been speaking to anyone in particular. CeCe often processed problems verbally to herself, it had always seemed to help her work through something that was particularly troubling.

She felt Cameron's hand on the small of her back, the small gesture so typical of a Dom, yet this touch seemed more like comfort than possession. "Love, you're good to go if you'd like to help. I have taken care of that part. You don't have to do anything. You are, after all, on holiday. But I'd heard about the local needs and well, quite frankly, I didn't think you'd be able to walk away from people who need you so desperately." He'd spoken so quietly, their conversation felt intimate and it was the first time she'd seen this level of compassion in his eyes. Having Carl back in his life had changed him. She suddenly realized there had always been a piece of his heart missing and Carl had returned it to him.

CeCe turned into Cam's embrace and hugged him fiercely. She hadn't realized until this moment how much she'd missed being a physician. Her life had been overtaken by administrative duties to the point she rarely connected with patients for more than a few moments. Without walking away and starting over, she would never be able to form the kind of community connections that really made a difference in people's lives. Oh sure, the surgical techniques she'd developed and taught to others would change lives for the better, but to impact an individual's life over a span of years as you shepherded them through trials and triumphs, that is what she'd always longed for. She wasn't sure where this newfound self-awareness would lead her, but she'd always believed that once your eyes were opened to something, it was foolish to close them again.

Turning to Carl, she hugged him and whispered against his ear, "Thank you for bringing the missing piece of his heart back to him." She felt him stiffen against her for just an instant before he hugged her back so hard she squeaked. When she turned back to Dr. Guzman, his wrinkled face bore a broad smile, "Well then, let's get to work."

"You are a manipulative bastard, you now that, right? You played that perfectly." Carl wasn't being critical and he was sure the humor in his voice made that clear to Cam. They'd said their goodbyes and were walking back to the overgrown golf cart Cam had called a car.

"I prefer to think of myself as an *outcome engineer*. It sounds so much better than manipulative bastard, even though in this case they are essentially one and the same."

"And I can't believe you call this fucking golf cart a car. Seriously, this thing is a joke. What if we need to out run the bad guys? Jesus, Fred, I don't think our bare feet will be able to keep up." Carl was only partially kidding about their mode of transportation. Hell, the thing looked like it belonged at some PGA tour stop. *I'm not usually a car snob, but Jesus Christ on a crutch this thing is just embarrassing.*

"Stop whining and get in. I'll show you exactly what this baby can do. Might want to fasten your safety harness, Barney." They spent the next several hours exploring the small island's roads, making note of various hiding places, and discussing the information Micah Drake had given them late last night. They spent time talking to several locals, asking them to make note of any strangers they saw and providing information on men Cam employed that they could trust. They'd also shown people Craig Allen's picture. It hadn't taken long to learn Cameron Barnes' name didn't carry much weight, until he pointed out Dr. Barnes was his wife.

"Do you even remember Allen? Hell, I've looked at those pictures a dozen times and I don't remember the man from St. Andrew's at all." Carl was baffled that someone from their old school was the one causing problems. And knowing he'd been working inside Dark Desires for so long was just fucking creepy. "And how the hell did he slip through your security screening?"

"Well, in answer to your last question, he was hired through an agency." And that was a mistake he wouldn't make again. "They would have screened for criminal history and the like. His education history wouldn't have flagged them because they wouldn't have had any way to know I'd gone to the same school. As for me remembering him, I didn't remember his name, but one of the pictures sparked a memory. He was a year or two behind us, but was in one of our computer classes. Easy to understand why he was in an advanced class after reading his file. Christ, and he'd been working as a fucking janitor? Presumably just to get close to me? What kind of sick shit is that? And if he'll go to that extent, what else is he capable of? My gut tells me this isn't going to end well, and that scares me. The only thing keeping me from putting the three of us on another plane is my trust in the team we've assembled."

Carl agreed with Cam's assessment, but he was still uncomfortable leaving CeCe at the clinic. Sure, they had people in place watching Allen, and the truth was they didn't have any hard evidence against the man, but the hair stood up on the back of Carl's neck every time the man's name was mentioned and he'd learned a long time ago to never discount his instincts. He didn't know Captain Andrews, but she hadn't hesitated to step up and put herself in danger when Jax had called her, so she'd earned a good deal of his respect from the start. And taking a picture of that yearbook had proven what good instincts she had, so he didn't think she was in over her head—at least not yet.

Shortly after five in the afternoon, Cameron drove them back to the small medical clinic. When they walked in the empty waiting room, the receptionist was wiping her eyes. Carl felt a fission of fear move through him and rushed to the desk. "Where is Dr. Barnes? Is she alright? What's happened? Why are you crying?"

He'd practically steamrolled the older woman, but she'd simply smiled. "She is fine. She's amazing in fact. She worked through more patients in an afternoon than we'd have been able to treat in a week, yet each one received her personal attention. She has scheduled procedures through the next ten days—and I mean each day for ten consecutive days. The woman is a medical machine and an answer to many of these family's prayers."

Carl sagged in relief as Cam chuckled, "Oddly enough, I'm not at all surprised," glancing at the woman's nameplate he smiled because obviously the receptionist was Dr. Guzman's wife, "In fact, I've seen Mrs. Guzman's reaction before. Our Cecelia is quite remarkable, so this won't be the last time you see this I assure you."

He knew Cam had intentionally referred to Cecelia as *ours*, they'd already discussed the fact there didn't seem to be any reason to hide who they were. The island was far too small for secrets and from what he'd seen; the people were very open-minded. Of course there was always the fact they'd discovered during their conversations with people in the small hamlets around the island that the doctor and his brother, who it turned out was the local constable, shared the woman sitting in front of them singing Cecelia's praises.

They'd no sooner arrived back at the beach house when both Carl's and Cam's phones rang at the same time as if they'd been synchronized by fate to keep them from caring for the bone tired woman who'd barely managed to walk through the door on her own. As they answered, CeCe gestured upstairs with a half-hearted wave of her hand, and they both smiled and nodded. Cam had decided they wouldn't tell her about Craig Allen until after dinner. It had been easy to see she was exhausted and Carl hoped she was going upstairs to rest. He and Cam spoke on the phone with various members of the team making plans and setting up the details of the investigation. Carl wasn't sure how long they'd been working when he heard raised voices from the open door he'd been standing beside. Before he could take in the scene on the beach below the house, he heard a woman's blood-chilling scream followed quickly by two gunshots. He was already running for the door with Cameron right on his heels.

Chapter Twenty-One

CeCe didn't remember the last time she'd been this physically exhausted but emotionally fulfilled. Even during those fog-filled first days of motherhood, she hadn't felt like this. For the first time in several years, she knew in her heart she'd actually made a difference in someone's life. Sure she had a wildly successful medical practice, she'd won countless awards for her groundbreaking techniques, and she'd reached a level of professional recognition she'd only dreamt of in the beginning, but she'd lost focus on *why* she'd wanted to became a doctor in the first place. After trudging up the stairs, she'd been too restless to nap so she'd taken a quick shower before pulling on shorts and a tank top and stepping out onto the balcony overlooking the white sand beach. Watching a man and woman who were standing down on the beach, CeCe realized they were the same people she'd seen getting in the taxi at the airport the first night they'd arrived in St. Maarten.

Now that she had a chance to study the man, CeCe was fairly certain he was one of the janitors at Dark Desires. She'd talked to him a couple of times about trivial things like the blasted heat and annoying traffic delays due to road construction, but she certainly didn't think they knew one another well enough for him to casually drop by to visit while on vacation. And really, what were the odds he'd just happened to end up on the beach outside their new home? Perhaps she'd been more tired than she realized because before she had the chance to consider the consequences, she was stomping down the stairs leading to the beach.

It was obvious the couple wasn't getting along, even though she wasn't close enough to make out what they were saying, the tone was easy enough to interpret, and their body language was telling as well. As soon as they saw her, the beautiful blond woman put her back to CeCe. *Shit, what was his name? Allen? Craig? Damn, I can't remember.* The closer she got to them the more certain she was, hell, she'd recognize his whiney-assed voice anywhere. CeCe heard the woman call him Craig as she approached, but his raised voice had drowned anything else the young woman had said. And what the hello was he doing cursing at the woman he was trying to get around. "Hey, you. Aren't you an employee of Dark Desires? The club's management has very strict guidelines for their employees, and even though you aren't at work I can't imagine them looking favorably on the way you are talking to your girlfriend."

The woman's head practically rotated on her slender neck and under different circumstances, CeCe might have found the next few seconds amusing. "Girlfriend? Oh fuck, no." The woman's eyes were wide and her horrified expression was unmistakable, obviously they weren't a couple, so why were they arguing outside the beach house?

"Fuck you, bitch. You don't have the right equipment to be interesting to me." Then the man's attention shifted to CeCe, and his sneer was enough to stop her in her tracks. "But you. Oh yes, you, Dr. Barnes, I am quite interested in you. I've tried to be subtle, but you just don't take a fucking hint, do you?" *What the hell is he talking about?* The second that thought went through her mind,

CeCe knew. He must have seen the realization in her eyes because he chuckled. His laugh reminded her of Snidely Whiplash and, even lost in a daze of exhaustion and fear, CeCe wanted to shake her head at the absurdity of her thoughts. *Jesus Pete, Cecelia, you are facing a man who obviously hates you, he's just pointed a gun at your face and you're thinking about a cartoon. Yes, indeed, the men in white jackets will be here shortly to drop a net over your crazy ass—or maybe they'll have to put the net back and use a bag to scoop up the pieces if Mr. Whiplash over there shoots you.* What had she been thinking coming out here without Cam or Carl? *Oh God, of all things in heaven and hell, if I live through this they are going to kill me.*

Cecelia had read about things like this, heard people talk about how time seemed to slow and every one of their senses seemed to amplify. She'd never fully understood what they'd meant until now. Everything around her came into crystal clear focus, colors were so vivid they almost shimmered. Her hearing had become so acute she heard the gulls off shore searching for their last meal of the day, the sloshing of the waves as they lapped against the shore, the forlorn sound of a boat's horn as it passed by in the distance. Her heart's frantic beating sounded like a bass drum pounding out a rapidly accelerating beat as it threatened to drown out everything else around her. "What do you want from me?" She hated that her voice had sounded so weak, but truthfully, it was nothing short of a miracle that she'd been able to speak at all.

"Are you kidding? Are you really that fucking stupid?" *Evidently, because I don't speak "crazy".* He was looking at her like he expected her to answer that ridiculous question. *Nope, not happening. The longer I can stall the better my chances of getting out of this alive.*

The woman Snidely had been arguing with was moving between them again and CeCe had the impression she was trying to protect her. She'd been introduced to the men providing security for the house, but she was certain she'd never met this woman before. *It's not like anyone is ever going to forget her—Holy Hopscotch she's gorgeous. Jesus, Cecelia, focus already. It's not like you aren't in enough trouble already. Christ, I'm even talking to myself. I really should have taken a nap.*

"Are you even fucking listening to me? Christ, how can Master Cameron stand to live with you? Hello? Earth to dip-shit doctor." Something snapped in CeCe and her spine straightened with a snap as she narrowed her eyes on him. "Oh, yeah. Cop an attitude with me and see where that gets you. Fuck me, Master Cameron deserves so much better. I'll love him far better than you ever could. He's just forgotten about his promise, that's all. When I remind him that he promised to show me how it was done, he'll forget all about grieving for you."

Yep, a few sandwiches short of a picnic, this one.

"I don't even care that Carl is here, I'll enjoy being the filling in that hot sandwich." He tilted his head to the side as if studying her. "I saw them, you know. That night at the school. I was the one who told the Dean. I didn't think Cameron would take the blame. I thought Carl would leave. And then when I tried to find him that summer, he'd already left for the military." He kept rattling on, but CeCe had tuned him out as she tried to figure out the strange hand signals the woman was making behind her back. *Shit, I have no clue what that means? What do I look like, some gang-banger?*

The man was waving his gun around gesturing wildly as he ranted his way through a fanatical tirade. And suddenly everything seemed like it had been switched to slow motion and happen simultaneously. Craig came back to himself and leveled the gun so that it was pointed right between her eyes, she saw his jaw muscles clench and the muscles in his hand quiver. There wasn't any doubt that he was going to pull the trigger and all CeCe could see in her mind was a mental picture of Cameron rocking little Chloe. They'd only been home from the hospital for a few days and CeCe had been so tired she hadn't heard the baby cry. She'd woken up because Cam wasn't by her side and she never slept well if he wasn't by her side. When she'd padded barefoot down the thickly carpeted hall, she'd found them in Cam's office. He was rocking her in his enormous office chair, talking sweetly to her about all the wonderful places he planned to take her. They were illuminated by a single lamp, an island of love in a sea of darkness, and CeCe had stood in the dark—just watching. Now, she knew she'd never get to watch as her little girl learned to ride a bike as her daddy proudly guided her along. She'd miss all Chloe's precious school performances and graduations. And she wouldn't get to see Cameron walk her down the aisle someday—all because this delusional asshat thought he had a chance with Cam.

There was an explosion of activity startling CeCe back to the moment. The woman yelled for her to run just as she launched herself toward Craig. CeCe heard an ear-piercing scream but didn't realize it had come from her until she realized her throat was burning. She heard the pop of a handgun being fired and a soft moan, then a split second later the crack of a rifle shot split the air. CeCe turned to look behind her as she was running and then froze. Both the man and the woman lay motionless on the sand. She couldn't move, it was if her feet were trapped in the warm sand. Carl's arms banded around her squeezing tightly, but she was grateful because her knees folded almost immediately. "Breathe, baby, please just take a breath for me." His words sent a soft wash of warmth over her cheek to settle right in her heart. "That's my girl. Now another."

The black dots that had been dancing in front of her eyes finally started to fade and she realized Mitch and Cam were both hovering over the woman who had just saved her life. "She saved me. She told me to run and then launched herself at him. I don't even know her. Why would she be willing to die to save me?" She didn't have a clear view of the beautiful blonde who had acted so bravely, but it seemed odd that both Mitch and Cam were yelling into their phones about ambulances. Triage. And the suspect being neutralized. Without even realizing she was speaking out loud, CeCe asked, "Neutralized? Why don't they just say dead? Wouldn't dead be easier? It's much clearer."

Carl still held her locked against his chest, she could feel his heart beating against her own. He chuckled softly, "You are right. It would be simpler, but since when does the military do anything the easy way? Old habits die hard, baby. And just so you know, I'm fairly certain Captain Andrews isn't dead. Although as crazy as Mitch is acting, I'm not sure she's doing very well. And just for the record? That's what American soldiers do each and every day. They put their lives on the line for people they don't know." On a cognitive level, CeCe knew what he'd said was true, but she'd never seen it up close, and it was the most humbling moment of her entire life. Just as that thought worked through her mind every thought faded as the rest of what he'd said soaked through her adrenaline-saturated mind. *What? She's alive? I'm a doctor for heaven's sake.*

Chapter Twenty-Two

Cam paced the small waiting room of the small medical center until he could do it with his eyes closed just by counting the steps. For the first time in his life, he understood the true meaning of fear. When he'd heard Cecelia's scream his blood had turned to ice, but the two shots that followed had nearly caused his knees to fold out from under him. Running had been pure reflex because that had been the only part of his brain that had been functioning. Cam had only been steps behind Carl—*damn, he still runs like the wind*—but he'd known when he saw her wrapped in his friend's arms she was fine. He'd only paused long enough to see Carl's quick signal indicating their woman was safe before moving to Captain Andrew's side.

Mitch Ames had made the shot of a lifetime. He'd been running toward the trio on the beach when he'd seen Craig Allen take aim at Cecelia. Mitch had seen in a microsecond what the rest of them saw clearly when they reviewed the security footage, Allen had every intention of killing Cecelia. Without breaking stride, he'd drilled Allen almost dead center in the forehead with the M14 he'd been carrying. *Hell, shooting that rifle requires precision under ideal conditions and making that shot while running down a fucking rock covered hill is unimaginable. The man is going to be a fucking legend among his peers.* What Mitch had done was nothing short of phenomenal and certainly explained why the Pentagon was pressuring the Wests to stop recruiting the cream of their crop.

During a video conference call with Kyle West and Micah Drake, both men had reviewed the tape calling it the "shot of a lifetime." He hoped to hell that it was the shot of Cecelia's lifetime because just the thought of her ever being in that kind of danger again was enough to send him into a panic. It was hard to believe the hero that had saved both women was standing in front of the small room's windows staring outside even though Cam knew the man wasn't seeing a thing. Mitch had been in the same parade rest position for hours, he'd barely moved a muscle and at times Cam had wondered if he was even breathing. The only time he'd even responded to a question was when Mrs. Guzman had asked him if he needed anything.

Carl stepped up beside Cam and nodded toward Mitch, "Is he doing okay?"

Cam sighed before responding, "He will be, but he's struggling. I've never seen anyone power through an adrenaline crash like he did. Hell, he barely blinked. After what he went through most people would be down for the fucking count, but there he stands—still as a damned statue." When the door to the waiting room opened, Cam wasn't all that surprised to see Kent West and Jax McDonald stalk into the room.

Cam had known they were coming, but the speed with which they'd managed the trip was damned impressive. Kyle had stayed home with Tobi and their children because, to quote his friend, "She's gonna be hell on wheels when she finds out what's happened and she wasn't invited to the party." The truth was Cecelia probably could have used Tobi's comfort, but he agreed that adding the fiery Mrs. West to the craziness already surrounding them would be like pouring gas on a raging fire.

Kent broke off and headed for Mitch while Jax joined him and Carl. "How's Aspen?"

"We haven't heard anything for a while. They don't have enough medical staff to keep sending someone out with updates." Jax nodded his head in understanding. "Truthfully, I can't see how it can possibly take this long. I know there was a lot of damage. Fuck the bullet splintered several ribs as it bounced around ripping holes in her organs. It's a fucking miracle the internal bleeding alone didn't kill her before the paramedics got her here."

"From what I hear, your wife is the reason she made it this far. The Prairie Winds' team and the U.S. government are both going to owe her—no matter how this ends."

Jax had been speaking softly, but Mitch had obviously heard him. "Aspen is alive. She is fighting like hell to stay that way. Her soul is seeking strength from those of us surrounding her, so please monitor your thoughts." Cameron knew the former Green Beret had been raised in the Bayou, and the rumor mill had often referred to his voodoo beliefs, but it had always simply been gossip until now. Jax had nodded and Mitch had returned his attention to the window.

They settled in for the wait and Cam was overwhelmed by the generosity of the locals. Just as they'd been warned, word spread quickly around the small island. Soon they were being inundated with food and drinks. Many came to stand outside and pray for the woman who had saved their new doctor. The steady influx of well-wishers made the time go faster, but Cam still wondered how Cecelia was holding up. Christ, at this point she'd been on her feet for almost forty-eight hours. He had no idea what was sustaining her except a soul deep dedication to helping others. Cameron knew about the stories surrounding his time in the military and the years he'd spent as a private operator. He wasn't overly smug about the success he'd had, but he also knew it was damned impressive. But he was in awe of what his wife was capable of. She'd pioneered surgical techniques that were used the world over and she'd steadfastly refused to reap any windfall profit from patents. She'd only submitted the applications for patents to keep others from reaping the benefits, claiming saving lives was her only priority. Cam found himself silently adding his voice to the prayers of those around him, pleading for the wellbeing of both women. It had been a long time since he'd spoken to a God he'd often thought didn't know he existed, but knowing there had to be something greater out there because having her in his life couldn't possibly have been a coincidence—he simply wasn't that lucky.

CARL TRIED TO stay busy greeting the locals and managing calls, anything to keep from reliving the terror that had filled him until he'd been able to hold CeCe in his arms. How she had managed to pull herself back from the edge of exhaustion to care for Aspen Andrews was something he'd never understand. Hell, he'd seen well-trained soldiers leveled by crashes after less. But she'd pushed past the exhaustion to care for Captain Andrews with a single-minded determination that earned her a whole new level of respect in Carl's view. Sure, he'd liked her on sight and even respected her simply because of the information he'd read in the report he'd been given back in Austin. But this? This was something else entirely—this was the respect of one *soldier for another.*

Two doors at opposite ends of the room opened at the same time, Captain Andrew's commanding officer, Lieutenant Colonel Brian Riggs stepped into the room just as CeCe moved through the door Carl knew led to the small medical center. And goddammit if Commander Riggs didn't make a beeline to CeCe before Carl or Cam could intercept him. "Dr. Barnes, it looks like my timing is perfect for once. I'm Lieutenant Colonel Riggs, how is Captain Andrews?"

CeCe looked a bit stunned for a moment, but she rallied quickly, "It's a pleasure to meet you, sir, although I wish it had been under different circumstances." Everyone in the room watched as she shook the man's hand and then stepped back to ensure their conversation wasn't seen as private. "Now, if you'd kindly move back a bit I'd like to address everyone at the same time, I've only got a few minutes and I don't want to waste them repeating the information several times." *Good for you, baby. You grab those reins with either hand or he'll steamroll you and you'll never even feel the bump.* How could he have forgotten how annoying CO's could be? Sure, the room might have plenty of former military personnel in it, but the woman with the power was a civilian and obviously no shrinking violet. Glancing over at Cameron, Carl saw the corners of his mouth twitching up and knew he was thinking the same thing.

Cecelia's voice was crystal clear as she addressed the room, without even a hint of the fatigue she had to be feeling. She patiently explained the details of Captain Andrews' injuries, how she and Dr. Guzman had managed to repair the multitude of holes and tears caused by the bullet and the slivered pieces of Aspen's ribs. Carl found himself lost in all the medical jargon but he'd plainly heard the hope in her voice. When Lieutenant Colonel Riggs demanded to know when Captain Andrews would be well enough to return to duty, CeCe had leveled a look at him that would have withered a Brigadier General, "I'm not God, sir. I am a physician, a very tired physician who on occasion can exhibit a bit of a snarky attitude if you are inclined to listen to my husband. I am not one of your underlings, so the tone will not serve you well here." Every former soldier in the room was suppressing a smile and several had coughed to cover up their snorts of laughter. When CeCe noticed their reactions and Riggs' shocked expression, her cheeks tinted a lovely shade of pink before she continued, "I promise I will keep you updated if you'll leave your contact information with Mrs. Guzman. Since St. Maarten's view of patient confidentiality is considerably more lenient than I'm used to, I will be able to share more information."

Carl and Cam moved toward CeCe, flanking her in what he felt certain would quickly become a signature move. She looked up at them, blinking several times as if she was trying to get her tired eyes to focus before she smiled. Cam turned her so she faced him, then tipped her chin up with his fingers, "I'd like for you to eat something before you go back in there, love." Carl noticed he hadn't asked her if she was hungry, he'd basically told her he wanted her to eat. When she slowly nodded, Cam turned her to Carl saying, "Take her over into the corner and don't let anyone close. I'll make her a small plate."

Leading her across the small room, Carl settled her on his lap. Mitch stepped in front of them and before Carl could protest, he leaned forward and pressed a chaste kiss to her forehead. Carl knew the move was part apology and part gratitude even though the man hadn't spoken a word.

Mitch stepped back, turned, spreading his legs apart and crossing his bulging biceps over his broad chest in a move clearly letting everyone know they would have to get through him before disturbing CeCe. Carl had suspected Mitch's interest in Aspen Andrews was something more than simply professional, but the look of relief that swept over his face as CeCe explained how optimistic she was had validated his suspicion.

Shifting his attention to the woman leaning against his chest, Carl shifted so he could look into her eyes as he spoke, "You amaze me. I cannot imagine how spent you must be, yet your humble recounting of what happened in that operating room barely hints at what I know you've been through."

"If my Master hadn't funded all the upgrades here in his attempt to persuade me to move my practice here—well, we'd have lost her. It wouldn't have mattered what we would have done, without some of the pieces they'd just set up we'd be dealing with a much different outcome." The dark circles under eyes were turning darker with every minute and he wondered how long it would be until her body simply refused to cooperate any longer. As a SEAL, Carl had learned how to push his body to its absolute limit, so he recognized the signs and Dr. Cecelia Barnes was getting very close to the edge.

CeCe was one of the most sensual women Carl had ever met, he'd felt drawn to her from the moment she'd walked into Cam's office. Hell, that was a lie—he'd practically fallen in love with her just from reading her profile on the way to Houston. But in this moment, having her curled up in his lap—trusting him to shelter her even if just for a few moments, sex was the furthest thing from his mind. Everything he'd ever learned about the responsibility of a Dom to care for his submissive came into crystal clear focus in that moment. Trusting their Dom when they are at their most vulnerable, no matter what's brought them to that point, is the greatest gift a submissive can give. All the kneeling, collars, and mind-bending orgasms in the world mean nothing without trust.

Cam pulled a chair around until he could sit down facing CeCe. The significance of the move might not have meant anything to her, but it spoke volumes to Carl. Cameron Barnes would always be an *operative*. It was in his blood. It was just who he was as a person. So watching him put his back to the room warmed Carl's heart. As one soldier to another, the move had clearly telegraphed his trust in Carl. It was tantamount to shouting to everyone in the room that they were partners. Setting that aside, Carl listened intently as Cam spoke quietly to CeCe. Carl could feel her relaxing in his hold and he understood how his friend's soothing tone and words were putting her at ease.

Carl doubted CeCe realized how much she'd eaten from her Master's hand, and how close she was to falling asleep in his arms. The fruit, meat, and cheese were going to serve her well for the next several hours, she'd get the short-term boost from the fruit's sugar and the longer-term benefits from the protein in the meat and cheese. Cam had given her just enough of a respite to revive her for the next couple of hours, and the glint in his eyes as he met Carl's gaze above her head told him the man had a plan to pull her back from that overly relaxed state as well. Carl hadn't seen that particular look in a long time, but he recognized it immediately—Cam was up to something and he was damned happy about it. *Yes, indeed. This ought to be fun to watch.*

Chapter Twenty-Three

CAMERON HAD ALWAYS loved feeding Cecelia from his hand. There was something very powerful about the connection between a Dominant and his submissive when the Dom was providing for one of the sub's most basic human needs. The unspoken message was "you are mine to care for, your needs are mine to meet" and he'd yet to see the simple act be powerfully effective. Over the years, Doms had often approached him for advice when they didn't feel as though they'd fully bonded with the sub in their care. Without fail, hand feeding the sub during aftercare had been his first recommendation. And even though they hadn't just shared a scene, there was no doubt his lovely slave was as vulnerable as he'd ever seen her.

Each bite had been a step closer to pulling her back from the emotional collapse he'd seen on the horizon. He'd spoken to her in the same soft tone he used with Chloe and wanted to smile when the mother responded in exactly the same way their daughter did—huge dark eyes focused on him, taking in every nuance of his facial expressions. They were both sponges when it came to human connection and he'd often envied them that particular ability. *How perfect it would be to be able to find happiness in such a simple act. To feel that level of connection to another human being, a bond that could chase away the coldest feeling of loneliness and alienation had to be a gift straight from God.*

The thing about human connections that had always fascinated him was that they require trials and tribulations in order to strengthen. He'd always reminded the Doms he had trained that it was much like friendship—those that were new and lacked shared experiences weren't as strong as those that had endured the highs and lows of life over the years. The same was true of a Dom's connection with his submissive, and he was about to shift gears with his beautiful slave. Pushing her right now was going to not only strengthen the ties between the three of them, it was also going to send a bolt of electric energy through her. He could see how close she was to falling into a blissful sleep, but he also knew that isn't what she needed. Oh, her body might need the sleep, but her heart and mind needed to return to Aspen Andrews' side. And even though he'd like nothing more than to lead the two people seated in front of him out the door, he wouldn't—at least not just yet.

"Now that you've eaten a bit, there is something we need to address." Cam had deliberately changed his tone from soothing to the formidable Dom CeCe was intimately familiar with. As long-term D/s relationships went, theirs had been a fairly simple transition, but he knew she'd recognize the switch and the phrase "something we need address" for exactly what it was—the prelude to a punishment for misbehavior.

Watching her eyes widen as her mind pulled back from the quicksand it had been slogging through. He'd taken her hand in his own, wrapping his fingers around her wrist served two purposes—first was the subtle act of bondage and it also let him monitor her pulse so he'd know when she'd reached that perfect state between fighting and surrender. He wanted her alert, not frightened. *Perfect.* "You put yourself in danger by going down onto the beach." She'd also endangered Captain Andrews, but he wasn't going to mention that—she'd come to that conclusion on her own. And they'd deal with her feelings of guilt about that when the time came.

"Endangering what belongs to your Masters is not acceptable, pet." Her breathing hitched and she shuddered. He deliberately used the plural, Masters, she needed to start seeing him and Carl as a united front. "This isn't the time or place to resolve this issue, but rest assured the topic will come up again." *Oh yeah, she's wide-awake now. Probably won't last long, but should sustain her for a few hours.*

"Now, it's probably time for you to return to your patient." When she nodded and started to get up from Carl's lap, he stopped her by tightening his hand around her wrist, "Love, just for the record, I'm incredibly proud of you. Your skills saved a young woman's life today. I'm sure her family and friends will be eternally grateful."

He smiled when Carl whispered, "I think Mitch is also very grateful." When Cam looked over his shoulder, the hulking man had turned his face toward Cecelia, he winked, gave a quick nod, and then resumed his position shielding them from the rest of the room.

She seemed to have settled a bit and this time when she moved to stand, he let her. But before she moved past him, she looked up through her dark lashes and in a voice that was barely more than a whisper, said "Thank you. I know what you've done. You know me so well, Master." He simply smiled down at her as she turned and walked past him. *She's a gift I didn't deserve.*

MITCH AMES WATCHED Dr. Cecelia Barnes disappear

through the doorway leading to the hospital's few rooms. He'd watched the small sub shift from frightened kitten into a tiger out on that beach. CeCe had gone to extraordinary lengths to save Aspen's life and it wasn't something he would ever forget. Thinking back on the first time he'd seen Aspen, Mitch could still remember every single detail—the way her hair tumbled around her shoulders like a silky gold cape. Hell, her hair shone so brightly despite the dim lighting in the room, she'd almost looked like an angel—a very naked, very aroused angel. She'd been tied to a St. Andrew's Cross in the main lounge, as a Dom he later learned was a local psychologist flicked the soft deer hide strips of a flogger over her. Mitch had moved closer, standing to the side, watching, studying her every reaction. The scene had been erotic as hell, but it had been clear the two weren't involved in a long-term relationship—and something about that pleased Mitch far more that it should have.

Several hours later, Kent had introduced him to Dan Deal, the Dom he'd watched flog the captivating blonde submissive right into subspace. Oddly enough, despite very divergent occupations and interests, they'd hit it off. They'd even shared a scene with Aspen Andrews the next night. Since neither of them had considered sharing outside a club setting, they'd both been surprised how easily the topic had come up after she'd been called back to active duty.

During the next two years, they'd kept in contact and that friendship had been one of the reasons Mitch had taken the job in Austin. They had also kept track of Aspen through Jax McDonald. When Mitch had found out the Wests were recruiting Aspen for this assignment, Mitch hadn't hesitated to hop the first flight to New York. That first night on the street, he'd seen a small flare of recognition in her eyes, almost as if she knew she should know him, but wasn't sure why. He'd have been offended if it hadn't been so easy to understand. Hell, his hair was much longer and his face had been painted with black paint to better blend into the shadows outside the Wests' building. But as she'd been laying on the beach, her blood soaking the sand around her, he'd seen her eyes flutter open for just a few seconds. He'd seen rather than heard lips whisper his name and in that moment he knew…she belonged to him.

CAM MADE HIS way around the room to Kent West's side and nodded his head toward the door. When the two of them were alone outside, Cam looked up at the stars and smiled. It had been a long time since he'd been able to stand outside and see the stars—far too long, and he'd forgotten how much he'd missed it. "Are you and Kyle interested in my proposal?" He'd shot them a deal on the club and penthouse that he didn't think they'd be able to pass up. In exchange for the low asking price, he'd retain a small percentage of ownership, all of his employees would keep their jobs, and Fischer would receive a hefty raise as well.

"Yes, we are interested—very interested actually, but I'm not satisfied with the price." When Cam's face turned quickly in his direction, Kent held up his hands in mock surrender. "Hold on, hear me out. I know you don't need the money, but we don't do business this way. We'll go over the details later because I want to know that your wife is fully on board first. Perhaps we can help find a buyer for her clinic because the damned thing is worth a fucking fortune from what I hear."

Cam couldn't hold back his soft chuckle, "It is, indeed. But I don't think it's going to be a problem for Cecelia to walk away from it when she has already seen how much she is needed here. The pace she'd set for herself has taken a far bigger toll on her than she realizes—and far larger than I should have ever allowed." He really did feel guilty for the fatigue he'd seen in her eyes the past several weeks, hell, she'd been practically walking in her sleep each night by the time she'd gotten home from her evening rounds at the hospital. "As long as my employees are taken care of, I'll be happy with whatever you come up with. I'm not trying to sound like a sap, but damn it, most of them have been with me since I opened the club."

He'd always paid his dungeon monitors—and paid them well. He'd realized from the start that having well trained people the members could rely on would save him far more than it could ever cost, and he'd never regretted the decision. As a matter of fact, when the Wests had asked for his input when they'd first started Prairie Winds, that was one of the first things he had advised them on. And as far as he knew they'd been happy with the way it had worked out as well—even though many of their employees were now doubling as contract operatives.

"You still in on helping with missions if your particular very broad set of skills fit the bill?"

Cam snorted a laugh at Kent's attempt at tact. "I will be if Carl stays. I won't ever leave my family unprotected—I've made too many enemies over the years." He paused for a long while and Cam was sure his friend was probably wondering if he was going to answer any of the unspoken questions that lay between them. Finally, taking a deep breath, he turned to Kent, "I'm hoping he'll stay and build a life with us here. I won't ask him to give up working for you, but I will ask that you never send us both out at the same time. Cecelia and Chloe both deserve better." When he paused to take a breath, he was surprised to hear Kent chuckle.

"You think that just because all the juicy details of your relationship with Carl weren't in the file we don't know how close you were? Christ, Cam, you know Micah Drake better than that. Hell the man probably knows what you'll be having for dinner a week from tomorrow, nothing gets past him." Cam knew his mouth had fallen open but he honestly didn't know why he was so surprised. "You know, I spent hours on a fucking plane to get here because one of my best friends in the world was in a panic about Captain Andrews, I'm missing my kids, and my damned brother just sent me a picture of our very naked wife tied to our bed." The man sighed and then narrowed his eyes, "Fuck, I ought to just shoot you just for the fun of it. I'm absolutely certain it would be therapeutic, even though I know Tobi would be righteously pissed on her friend's behalf. What CeCe sees in your grumpy ass baffles me." Kent seemed to relax a bit after his mini-tirade, hell, Cam had never seen the normally calm twin so unhinged. "Want a bit of advice here? Fuck it, you're getting it regardless. Suck it up, admit how much you care about Carl Phillips, and get on with your life. You and I both know walking away has haunted you for years. We've known the two of you had a physical relationship for years, but only got the details of how it ended when we first started our club. And that was because we wanted to know everything about you before we asked for your help. Sure you and Jax had been friends for a long time, but you'd encountered a lot of shit over the years," he shrugged apologetically, "and we wanted to make sure none of it had stuck. No sense in us patterning ourselves after someone who was going to take us down like the Titanic at some point. So get off you hypocritical high horse and do what you need to do."

Cameron was shocked. Completely and utterly blown away. The truth of Kent's words hit him full force and he couldn't even imagine what an ass he must look like to his friends. He hadn't actually lied to any of them, but he'd damned well lied to them by omission and he hated to think how many punishments he'd meted out over the years for that very thing. And worst of all, he'd lost years with the only man he'd ever loved, because his idiocy wasn't restricted to just the last few years. No, that particular affliction had started that night twenty-five years ago. Christ he had a lot to make up for.

As if he knew how thrown off Cam was feeling, Kent slapped him on the back before saying, "I'll tell you what, you yank your head out of your ass and figure out what kind of commitment ceremony you'd like and we'll host it. Of course we're going to turn Tobi and Gracie loose on your ass, they'll run you ragged with calls and texts about the details." Kent leaned his head back and laughed at what Cam knew was a stricken look on his face. Hell, he was all-in about the commitment ceremony, but being subjected to the two whirlwinds subs that terrorized Prairie Winds was just terrifying.

Kent laughed again, "Yes, indeed. This ought to go a long way in evening out the score. Don't ever assume your friends are idiots just because they don't throw the secrets you are trying ineffectively to hide back into your face. And don't get a stick up your ass thinking they'll judge you, that's just plain insulting. Now that I know Aspen is going to be okay, I'm anxious to get home. We'll hang around until she wakes up but then Jax and I will be heading out." Cam was surprised when the man pulled him in for a hug before pounding him on the back. Pulling back, he looked directly into Cam's eyes, "Don't fuck this up, Barnes, you have everything at your fingertips. Don't let it slip away again." *Wise words from a man who'd seen some of humanities worst and appeared to have come through it unscathed.* The wear and tear on a soul showed in Kyle on occasion, but Kent always seemed to live in the moment, a habit Cam hoped very much to cultivate in himself.

As they stepped back into the small waiting room, Cam realized he actually felt lighter, as if the weight of the world had been lifted from his shoulders. He wondered if it showed in his face when Carl looked up, surprise registering in his expression before he raised a brow in question. Cam couldn't hold back his smile—Christ, how long had it been since he smiled *just because?* For years he'd worried someone might uncover his secret and use it against him only to discover it hadn't been a secret for a long time—there was something very liberating in that. And knowing his reputation as an operative and as a Dominant hadn't been diminished by his friends' discovery was empowering. He'd been looking forward to making changes in his family's life, but now he could hardly wait and the anticipation had him practically dancing on the balls of his feet.

When Cecelia stepped through the door an hour later to let them know Aspen was awake and talking, the room erupted into joyful chaos and he wrapped her in his arms and twirled her around in a circle. "Well done, pet. I can't begin to tell you how proud I am of you, even though Uncle Sam will probably be trying to recruit you now." She grinned up at him even though he knew his sudden public display of affection had surprised her. *And that is another thing I need to change. My family needs to know that I love them, no matter where we are.* His days as the cold and distant man he'd become over the years were numbered. He was wise enough to know he wouldn't change overnight, but he felt like he was emerging from a dark tunnel into the light of day for the first time since he'd walked away from Carl that night at St. Andrew's.

"Thank you, Master." Her soft voice warmed him from the inside out, but the uncertainty he heard in her tone told him just how far he had to go before he'd be the man he wanted to become. After pressing a soft kiss to her forehead, Cam turned her into Carl's arms and watched as the only two people he'd loved as an adult, embraced one another. As soon as his daughter joined them the four of them could begin building their lives together, and Cam could hardly wait. But first, his sweet slave had the paddling of her life coming for putting herself in danger and scaring ten years off his life, but this punishment would be unlike any other she'd ever gotten. The scene he had planned wasn't going to be a Master's reminder to a slave, this time it was all about reminding the sweet submissive who had entrusted herself into his care, that she was equally responsible for the protection of what belonged to him…and to Carl. It might have been accidental, but their trifecta was going to end up being the best gift Cameron Barnes had ever received.

Epilogue

Six Months Later…

LARA LEANED AGAINST the fireplace mantle, surveying the room. The office Peter and Fischer Weston shared at Dark Desires had been completely transformed since the day her entire life had done a one-eighty six months ago. That day she'd been interviewed for a nanny position by her boss—a job she'd gotten, but never performed. Cameron and Cecelia Barnes insisted she had indeed lived up to her obligation, but that was just smoke and mirrors in Lara's opinion. Good God Gertie, babysitting for a few hours on two different evenings so your boss could play at the club did not qualify you as a nanny. And those two evenings playing with the cutest little girl Lara had ever seen certainly didn't merit the ridiculous sum of money they'd paid her. But when Lara had started to protest, her former boss had threatened to inform her Masters she was being insolent and then sit back and enjoy watching her punishment. *The rat bastard would have done it too. I don't care how much everyone says he's mellowed, I saw the old Master C—eyes flashing fire and pure male dominance.*

She had finally relented, but she'd happily joined forces with Tobi and Gracie when they'd been tasked with organizing the Barnes and Phillips commitment ceremony. She couldn't have asked for a more entertaining pair of co-

conspirators, they'd made so many FaceTime calls Lara had to add time to her cell plan, but being able to torture Master C with trivial details had made the expense worth every cent.

Pulling back the heavy drapery covering the window that looked down into the club's main room, she couldn't hold back her smile. How Tobi and Gracie had managed to transform a room filled with BDSM equipment into what now resembled an English garden with a side of kink was a mystery for the ages. When she felt a strong arm encircle her waist she squeaked in surprise, she knew in an instant it was Peter. Even though he claimed to have spent most of his time as a SEAL supplying the teams with information, she wasn't buying it—the man moved like a ghost. Tobi and Gracie had laughed when Lara had complained about getting caught grumbling to herself behind his back. Both women had assured her it was just one of the curses of dealing with former operatives, and then proceeded to recount some of their own mistakes. Lara had ended up laughing so hard she'd been mopping tears from her eyes.

"Penny for your thoughts, precious. Care to share what's put that Mona Lisa smile on your sweet lips?" Peter's sweet words moved over the shell of her ear leaving behind heat far more intense than the warmth of his breath. They had all three been so exhausted each night the past week by the time they'd returned to the penthouse, they'd barely had the energy to shower before falling face first into bed and her body was beginning to protest the lack of attention. But after tonight's ceremony, Lara intended to have her wicked way with her Masters, even if it meant getting a few swats beforehand.

"My love, you know even though I can't hear your thoughts clearly that doesn't mean I'm not getting very strong emotions. Anytime we are skin to skin I'm gifted with awareness of what you are feeling, and right now I'm feeling a bit neglected." She couldn't hold back her gasp of surprise, *damn it all to dirty dominos. How did he know?* When she'd met his grandmother, the older woman had warned her that as their bond grew, both men's abilities to "read her" would probably strengthen as well, but she'd shrugged it off as something to worry about a few years into the future rather than just a couple of months. *Frack a big friggin' frog.*

Peter moved so quickly she barely had time to register the movement before she felt two heated swats on her thinly covered ass. The dress they'd chosen for her to wear was made of midnight blue silk and was the most comfortable thing she'd ever worn—except for the fact it was cut to her naval in the front and to the dimples at the top of her ass in the back. When she'd asked how she was supposed to keep her breasts from making a sudden appearance both men had simply shrugged. She was guessing they wouldn't be too happy about the double stick tape she'd used to secure the edges. Lara quickly banished those thoughts hoping Peter hadn't picked them up.

"I was looking down over the room and couldn't help but grin at the way Tobi and Gracie have managed to change the entire feel of the room. They didn't really move any of the equipment out or hide it from view, they just added so many softer elements that your eyes don't focus on the black leather, hanging chains, and wooden St. Andrew's Crosses." She snickered when she realized everything was still in plain sight, just camouflaged.

Peter's chuckle vibrated his chest against her bare back and she felt her pussy flood with liquid need. "Well, suffice to say, Cam and Carl are worried they're going to both have—and I quote, 'floral induced seizures' before the ceremony is over. Kent laughed, blaming Cam for letting the two defiant subs know he wasn't a big fan of roses." Lara laughed because she knew that was exactly why the two women had ordered thousands of flowers as decorations. "Did you know we had to send a truck to the airport this morning to get the last *shipment*? I shudder to think what kind of bill they'll be presenting him with." Lara knew but she wasn't going to cop to it, and she fully intended to make herself scarce before her two friends dropped *that* bomb. It wasn't that he couldn't afford it, but she was fairly certain Master Cam was going to play along just the same because truthfully, both women would be terribly disappointed if he didn't kick up a big fuss.

Peter squeezed her tightly before nuzzling her neck, "Don't worry, Carl has already briefed Cam on the importance of acting annoyed, even though my brother swears neither Tobi nor her band of pirates could have done anything to spoil his mood today." Lara giggled, she'd forgotten that Tobi's mother-in-law, Lilly West, had joined in on most of the planning sessions. And talk about a pirate, holy hell, Lilly was a wild child despite being almost sixty years old. Tobi swore that every woman who knew Lilly wanted to "be her" when they grew up, and Lara was sure it was true.

Lara heard the door open just before Fischer spoke, "Hey, stop pawing her, she's got to look perfect for the ceremony."

"Leave it to Mr. Fashion Statement to care more about wrinkling your dress than getting a chance to feel your softness under his fingertips. Your spa days are worth their weight in gold, my beautiful *amore*." Regular visits to the club's spa had been one of the first *rules* they'd put in place for her. Lara was sure that it had started out as a way for them to teach her the importance of taking care of what belonged to them, but they had never made any secret of how much they enjoyed the benefits as well.

"Come on you two, our guests are arriving and the sooner we get this show on the road the sooner we can go home and play. Personally, I can hardly wait to give our sweet cupcake a paddling for trying to use tape to keep her breasts concealed from our view." Both men chuckled at her surprised gasp.

Well, fuckity fuck, how did they know? The thoughts had no more than moved through her mind than both men burst out laughing as they escorted her out of the room.

The End

Books by Avery Gale

The Wolf Pack Series
Mated – Book One
Fated Magic – Book Two
Tempted by Darkness – Book Three

Masters of the Prairie Winds Club
Out of the Storm
Saving Grace
Jen's Journey
Bound Treasure
Punishing for Pleasure
Accidental Trifecta
Missionary Position

The ShadowDance Club
Katarina's Return – Book One
Jenna's Submission – Book Two
Rissa's Recovery – Book Three
Trace & Tori – Book Four
Reborn as Bree – Book Five
Red Clouds Dancing – Book Six
Perfect Picture – Book Seven

Club Isola

Capturing Callie – Book One

Healing Holly – Book Two

Claiming Abby – Book Three

I would love to hear from you!

Email:

avery.gale@ymail.com

Website:

www.averygalebooks.com/index.html

Facebook:

facebook.com/avery.gale.3

Instagram:

avery.gale

Twitter:

@avery_gale

Made in the USA
Columbia, SC
03 July 2017